# BIGGLES DELIVERS THE GOODS

'It will be better for you if you talk freely,' promised the officer.

'I know, but I prefer to say nothing,' returned Algy.

Upon this there was a brief conversation between the interpreter and the senior officer.

Addressing Algy again the interpreter inquired, 'Where do you go and why do you carry petrol?'

'I have already told you that I have nothing more to say,' answered Algy. 'In that, as you know quite well, I am within my rights as a prisoner of war.'

There was another conversation in Japanese.

'It will be bad for you if you do not answer questions,' said the interpreter.

Algy nodded. 'I know.'

'You will say nothing?'

'Nothing. I have told you all that I am compelled to tell you.'

'You will be sorry.'

'No,' stated Algy. 'Whatever you do I shall not be sorry.'

# BIGGLES DELIVERS
# THE GOODS

## CAPTAIN W. E. JOHNS

**RED FOX**

Red Fox would like to express their grateful thanks for help in
preparing these editions to Jennifer Schofield, co-author of
*Biggles: the life of Captain W. E. Johns,* published by Veloce
Publications, Linda Shaughnessy of A. P. Watt Ltd and
especially to John Trendler, editor of *Biggles & Co,* the quarterly
magazine for Biggles enthusiasts, the address of which may be
found at the back of this book.

A Red Fox Book

Published by Random House Children's Books
20 Vauxhall Bridge Road, London SW1V 2SA

A division of Random House UK Ltd
London Melbourne Sydney Auckland
Johannesburg and agencies throughout the world

© W. E. Johns 1946

First published by Hodder & Stoughton 1946
Red Fox edition 1994

Set in Baskerville Roman by Intype, London
Printed and bound in Great Britain by
Cox & Wyman Ltd, Reading, Berkshire

RANDOM HOUSE UK Limited Reg. No. 954009

ISBN 0 09 939441 3

# Contents

# Chapter 1
# An Unexpected Visitor

When Biggles—Squadron Leader James Bigglesworth, D.S.O., D.F.C.,* to give him his proper name and rank—when Biggles was informed by 'Toddy', the Station Adjutant,** that Air Commodore Raymond of Air Intelligence had been on the telephone, requesting his presence forthwith at the Air Ministry to meet an old acquaintance, he hazarded several guesses as to who it might be. None was right. In fact, as he subsequently admitted to Algy Lacey, had he made as many guesses as an airscrew turns during a three-hour sortie, he would still have been wrong.

His arrival at Air Intelligence Headquarters was followed by a procedure so unusual as to mystify him further. Instead of being shown direct into the Air Commodore's private office, as was customary, he was taken by a messenger to an ante-room where he was requested to wait, and where, presently, Air Commodore Raymond, Deputy Director of Air Intelligence, joined him. No time was wasted in idle conversation. As soon as greetings had been exchanged, seats taken and cigarettes lighted, the Air Commodore gave Biggles

---

* Distinguished Service Order, Distinguished Flying Cross, two Air Force medals
** The officer in charge of assisting the Commanding Officer

the answer to the question that had exercised his mind all the way from the station to the Ministry.

'Did you ever, in your travels, meet a Chinaman named Li Chi?' he inquired.

Biggles was so taken aback that he made no attempt to conceal his astonishment. He stared blankly at the Air Commodore for a full ten seconds before he answered. 'Why—er—yes . . . as a matter of fact I did. It was a long time ago though.'

The Air Commodore nodded. 'The Chinese have long memories.'

'Evidently. I'd forgotten the existence of the fellow.'

'He hasn't forgotten you, apparently.' The Air Commodore leaned forward, eyes questioning. 'What do you know about him?'

'Very little,' replied Biggles cautiously. 'He was educated in this country, finishing at Oxford. Speaks English as well as I do—better, maybe. Plenty of money. He told me on the one occasion that we met that his father was a wealthy merchant in Shanghai. Li Chi was not his real name; actually it's the name of a Chinese fruit; but it was the name by which he was known from the China Sea to the Bay of Bengal. I won't say he was a crook because crook is an ugly word; but he was a smuggler in a big way of business. His special line was running opium into India. He had a nice sense of humour, understood the meaning of gratitude, and must have known the seaboards and islands of the Indian Ocean better than any man on earth. That's all.'

The Air Commodore gave Biggles a curious look. 'How did you come to meet this unusual individual?'

Biggles smiled. 'I don't know that I care to tell you.'

'Why not?'

'No man need give evidence that may subsequently be used against him.'

'Don't be so infernally evasive. Just what do you mean?'

'I was once an accessory—an innocent accessory, I must say in fairness to myself—to a crime.'

'What was the crime?'

'Helping a man to escape from the long arm of British law.'

'A criminal!'

'No. You can't say that. He was never brought to trial, so was never convicted. Say *alleged* criminal, if you like.'

'I imagine there wasn't much doubt about it?' said the Air Commodore drily.

Biggles' smile broadened. 'You're quite right—there wasn't.'

'Tell me what happened,' invited the Air Commodore.

Biggles hesitated. 'It's a longish story.'

'No matter—tell me. I have good reasons for asking.'

'Very well. Here, as brief as I can make it, is the yarn.* About 1934 or '35—speaking from memory—I was flying home from the Far East in an amphibious aircraft** named the Vandal. Algy Lacey was with me. At that time we were freelance civil pilots and had been East on a private venture. Coming up the coast of Malaya, on the run from Penang to Rangoon, we saw a raft floating on the sea, with a body on it. We

* This adventure appears as a short story in *Biggles Flies Again*.
** An aircraft able to land on sea or land

went down. The body turned out to be that of a Chinaman. He wasn't dead, but he was all in. After we had brought him round he told us that his name was Ho Sing. His junk* had been sunk—so he said—by the notorious pirate Li Chi. I wanted to push on to Rangoon and suggested taking him there, but he offered me five thousand Malay dollars to take him first to Penang and then on to an island of the Mergui Archipelago, where his crew had been marooned. As you probably know, the Archipelago is strung out along the west coast of the Isthmus of Malaya and Lower Burma, so it wasn't far out of my way. I accepted his offer, put him ashore on the island, collected my fee and went on to Rangoon, where I got a nasty shock. I learned that Li Chi had been captured a few days earlier by a British sloop, the *Cormorant*, Captain Starkey, R.N. But Starkey couldn't hold his man. After dark Li Chi took a header into the sea and got away. He took a sporting chance with his life, for if the Vandal hadn't come along he would have died.'

'You mean—?'

'The man I picked up was not Ho Sing. It was Li Chi himself—no less. I swallowed his fiction story about Ho Sing like a kid sucking an orange.'

'Are you sure of this?'

'Quite sure. You see, when I left Ho Sing—as he called himself—he gave me a packet, not to be opened until I reached Rangoon. When I opened it I found inside a pair of superb pink pearls, with a note thanking me for my kindness. It was signed Li Chi. Algy was

---

* A flat-bottomed Chinese sailing boat, sometimes also fitted with an engine

there—he'll confirm it. As a matter of detail we sub-sequently sold the pearls in Paris for £8,000, which provided us with some badly needed pocket money. We were within our rights. The pearls were a present. The fact that the donor was a wanted man made no difference. There was no indication that the pearls had been stolen. Li Chi's legitimate business in the islands was pearling, so I was satisfied in my mind that they had come from the bed of the sea, and not from a stolen necklace. Anyway, I ascertained that Li Chi paid the Indian government for his pearling concession. There was no humbug about that. His smuggling activities were a sideline, and I'm inclined to think he did it as much for sport as for any other reason. He didn't really need money. Now you know what I meant when I said he had a sense of humour and appreciated gratitude. He must have laughed up his sleeve at the way the two English simpletons accepted his yarn about Ho Sing.'

'What did you do about this at the time?'

'Frankly, nothing. For one thing it was no business of mine. I was not even a serving officer, much less a policeman. And secondly, you may be sure that I did not want to advertise the fact that I'd been sold a pup.* Had the story got out I should have been the laughing stock of every aero club between London and Singapore.'

'Sounds like bribery and corruption to me.'

'Nothing of the sort,' protested Biggles. 'The pearls were not a bribe. By the time I had received them the job had been done and he was clear away. He need

* Slang: been fooled

11

not have given them to me. The fact that he did reveals a sense of genuine gratitude. If it comes to that he needn't have given me the promised five thousand dollars for putting him on the island. His crew were there. There was nothing to prevent Li Chi from making his escape secure by murdering the pair of us and scuttling our aircraft. As it was he took a risk of our telling the authorities where he was hiding. Maybe that's another reason why we kept our mouths shut about the affair. I never saw him again, nor heard of him. Well, now you know the whole story, what about Li Chi?'

'He's here.'

'*Here!*'

'In my office.'

'Under arrest?'

'Not exactly. He gave himself up at Calcutta two months ago—but not, you may be sure, from any feeling of remorse or desire to do penance. Whatever else he may or may not be, he's a Chinaman, and to say that he hates the Japs for what they have done to China is to express his feelings mildly. He says—and it may be true—that the Japs in Shanghai decapitated his father for refusing to give them certain information. When you kill a parent in a country where ancestor worship is a religion, you start something, and I imagine that Li Chi's one ambition in life now is to do a spot of decapitating himself. Actually, he came to us with an idea which he thinks will annoy the Japs and at the same time do us a bit of good.'

Biggles drew a deep breath, a light of understanding in his eyes. 'Ah! I get it,' he breathed. 'What's the big idea about?'

'A certain war* commodity—one which at this moment is nearly worth its weight in gold—rubber. Come in and have a word with him yourself. He claimed that he knew you, and I was anxious to confirm that this was a fact before I brought you together. I know you have some odd friends scattered up and down the globe—'

'While men are decent to me I try to be decent to them, regardless of race, colour, politics, creed, or anything else,' asserted Biggles curtly. 'I've travelled a bit, and taking the world by and large, it's my experience that with a few exceptions there's nothing wrong with the people on it, if only they were left alone to live as they want to live.'

'All right—all right,' said the Air Commodore soothingly as he got up. 'Let's go and see Li Chi.'

Biggles renewed acquaintanceship with the man who had so neatly beguiled him, with a smile that was friendly, but held a suspicion of reproach. The Chinaman, immaculately dressed in European style, was not in the least embarrassed. He too, smiled—the elusive, enigmatic smile of the Orient that might mean anything. Rising from the chair in which he had been seated he bowed from the waist.

'That we should meet once was written in the Book of Fate,' he said gravely, in smooth, polished English. 'That our paths should cross again is an honour I do not deserve.'

'I'll reserve my opinion until I see the outcome of the meeting,' returned Biggles cautiously. 'Life has

* This story is set in the later years of the Second World War

treated you kindly. You haven't aged a day since I last saw you.'

'We Chinese grow old slowly,' answered Li Chi simply. 'You too, have carried the years well, if I may say so without impertinence.'

'When you've finished handing each other bouquets, suppose we get down to business,' suggested the Air Commodore. 'Be seated, gentlemen.' He looked at Biggles. 'Mr Li Chi has a plan. He has already talked with me about it. I will now ask him to repeat it, so that we may have your opinion of it.'

Biggles turned to Li Chi. 'Please proceed. Knowing the East as you do, anything you say will be worth hearing.'

'Thank you,' acknowledged Li Chi. Sitting back, with his fingers together, he went on. 'Britain needs rubber. Before the war most of the rubber of commerce came from Malaya.* Now Japan has captured Malaya** there is not as much rubber available for the Allies as they would wish.'

'That is something all the world knows,' assented Biggles.

'My plan is to provide Britain with rubber from Malaya,' said Li Chi blandly.

Biggles waited for a moment. 'Go on.'

'That is all.'

'You have not forgotten that the Japanese occupy Malaya, that they, too, need rubber, and would object strongly to our sharing it with them?'

* Now Malaysia
** Japanese forces attacked Malaya, a British colony in 1941, rapidly defeating British and Allied forces during the following weeks

'I have not forgotten. They will not miss what they do not know exists.'

'You think Malayan rubber can be made to vanish into thin air?'

Li Chi smiled. 'Thin air, or thick—it does not matter which, as long as an aeroplane can fly through it.'

'I see,' murmured Biggles thoughtfully. 'You have a plan for collecting rubber in Malaya and transporting it by air to India, or some other convenient place?'

Li Chi bowed. 'Precisely.'

'Now, suppose you tell us just how this is to be accomplished,' requested Biggles.

# Chapter 2
# Li Chi Outlines his Plan

'In considering the plan I will ask you to keep in mind certain factors, factors which alone could make the project feasible,' said Li Chi. 'First, there are in Malaya a million Chinese coolies,* workmen, who will help us. Every one of them will obey my orders, to death if necessary. Secondly, I know the country from Rangoon to Singapore, as I know my face. I know every island off the coast, although there are hundreds. I know the Indian Ocean, every current in it and every wind that blows. I even know the bed of the sea, for I have walked on it, seeking pearls. In short, I am well equipped with all the information that such a scheme as mine demands.'

A slight frown creased Biggles' forehead. 'I agree— but haven't you been rather a long time discovering this?'

'Your question is reasonable. I should have told you that when the war began, I returned to China to stand by the side of my honourable father. I was too late. He was dead, brutally murdered by the invading barbarians, against whom I at once resolved to wage war in my own way. To do this I returned by easy stages to my old haunts in the Mergui Archipelago.'

'Wasn't that rather like entering the lion's den,

* Oriental labourers

considering that most of the islands are only ten or twelve miles from the coast of Malaya?'

Li Chi opened his hands, palms upwards. 'My dear sir, with hundreds of islands from which to choose a hiding place, the Japanese could no more catch me than they could catch the man in the moon. But allow me, please, to finish. From the islands I struck at my enemies, and if I told you how many heads have fallen to the *parangs*\* of my commandos, how many Japanese have died from the poisoned dart, you would think me guilty of exaggeration. And all this time, to prevent the Japanese from having it, and perhaps to enrich myself at the same time, rubber has flowed in a steady stream from the mainland to the islands, where I have hidden it so that it will not be found. I have not less than five thousand tons so hidden, and this amount could be increased.'

'How did you move that quantity without being spotted?'

'Obviously it was not shipped as a single cargo. It came to me a few pounds here, a few pounds there. When a hundred thousand coolies are secretly tapping the trees,\*\* and stealing in small quantities from the Japanese dumps, the ultimate volume is considerable. Small packages are passed from hand to hand to the coast under the eyes of the invader. Even if he knew of this he would be powerless to prevent it unless he slaughtered every coolie in Malaya, which he dare not do, for it would leave him without skilled labour. Sometimes, of course, a man is caught. He dies with sealed

---

\* A large, heavy knife, used by the Malays as a weapon
\*\* Extracting the liquid from the trees, from which rubber is made

lips. Another takes his place. One cannot control an army of ants. Our enemies might as well try to stop the tide of the sea as prevent the leakage of rubber to the coast.'

'And then?'

'Little by little it crosses the narrow sea to my island, in canoes, in *prahus**, in *kabangs**, paddled over by Dyaks, by Malays, and Tamils, and Salones—those nomads who are called gipsies of the sea.'

'Are they paid for this?'

'No. Their reward is the hurt they do to the brutal Japanese.'

'I see,' murmured Biggles. 'It boils down to this. You have a quantity of rubber. You can get more, and you are willing to sell it to the British government?'

Li Chi frowned. 'Not sell. Give. In return I only ask that my past transgressions should be forgotten.'

'Just a moment,' interposed the Air Commodore. 'I have spoken to the Treasury about that. They thank you for your generous offer, but His Majesty's government does not accept favours of that sort. It will buy the rubber at an agreed price. That will allow you to recompense the coolies without touching your own money.'

Li Chi bowed. 'It shall be as you wish.'

'And we are to transport the rubber by air to India, the nearest British territory?' resumed Biggles.

'Yes. By air is the only way,' answered Li Chi. 'Japanese aircraft patrol the coast. A junk, or any seagoing craft, would be seen and intercepted.'

'It's a long way from the Archipelago to India.'

* Small native boats

'Twelve hundred miles, whether you take a course west for Ceylon or north-west for Calcutta. But if my knowledge is correct there are planes that could make the round trip?'

'Yes, that is so.'

'Then all that will be needed is a safe mooring at the islands, and that, I think, I could provide. I may say that I have other plans, but they come into the general scheme which we have discussed. For example, I have spoken with Major Marling, with whom I have for some time maintained a strange friendship. He is willing to help us. For years I have been his only link with the civilisation he so long ago renounced.'

'Who is this Major Marling?' asked Biggles. He glanced at the Air Commodore, who shook his head to signify that he knew nothing of him.

A ghost of a smile hovered for a moment about Li Chi's thin lips. 'Major Marling is an unusual member of that unusual race—the English. There are some in the Malay States who assert that he is not right in the head. They may be correct, but who in this war-crazed world is to say which of us are sane and which are insane?'

'What has this man to do with us?' asked the Air Commodore shortly.

Li Chi answered: 'Twenty years ago Major Marling was one of the most popular officers of the British army in India. He was handsome, wealthy—but not wise, for he committed the most unpardonable indiscretion in the eyes of the authorities which a British officer in India can commit. He fell in love with a local girl—a princess to be sure, but still, a girl of the country. There was a scandal, as a result of which he was invited to

19

resign his commission*—an invitation which he was bound to accept. Then, in the face of the powers that be, he married the girl. He could not stay in India. He would not return to England. So with his beautiful young wife he retired to the most inaccessible part of Lower Burma, a tract of land reached only by a dangerous river. There he established his home, and in time, a little colony. He did not remain idle; he developed the land and made it productive, to the great benefit of those who worked for him. Among other things he has a large rubber plantation and a ruby mine. For twenty years he has remained buried in the jungle, and in all that time he has not seen a single white man. Visitors were turned away at the boundary of his estate. As the years went on he inclined more and more to the way of life, the clothes and habits, of those about him, with the result that until a short while ago it is doubtful if anyone would realise that he was an Englishman. Then, soon after the war began, prompted perhaps by a whim, or pride of race, or it may have been by a sudden burst of patriotism, or defiance to the enemy, he resumed his British nationality—in his dress and his mode of life.'

'Wasn't that an indiscreet move?' queried Biggles.

'So I thought, and I told him so. But Major Marling is a law unto himself. Once his mind is made up he accepts advice from no man; he as good as told me to mind my own business. But to continue. His wife died a long time ago, but she gave him a son who is called Prince Lalla. The title may be a courtesy one, or it may be that as his mother was a princess in her own

---

* Give up his position in the army

20

right the son is entitled to princely rank. I do not know. The subject is one I have never cared to raise with the major. It does not matter. Prince Lalla lives with his father at Shansie, the name of the estate. All he knows of western civilization is from what he has read in books. He was taught English by his father, who is called by his people, Bhatoo. He is now getting on in years, but he still rules the estate with a rod of iron. Nevertheless, he is much loved, and is venerated by his people, to whom he is a father. The enemy invasion of Malaya and Burma did not cause him to leave the country. The Japanese demanded that he send them his rubber, and he does, in fact, send a certain amount to save himself from molestation; but the bulk of what he produces is hidden in the jungle. We may have it if we can fetch it.'

'Extraordinary tale,' murmured the Air Commodore. 'And you are in touch with him?'

'Yes.'

'What are his feelings now towards Britain? Would he help us if he could?'

'Of course. Before the war it amused him to help me to cheat the government which he always felt had used him badly. I sold rubies for him in an illegal manner. But that is of the past. Like me, he has become more conscious of his nationality.'

'Tell me,' put in Biggles, 'how did you get to India from the islands?'

'In a boat. There was no other way.'

'What sort of boat?'

'A native *kabang*. A larger vessel would have been stopped by a Japanese patrol, had it been seen.'

21

'Twelve hundred miles in an open boat was a tall order.'

'Not to a man who has spent his life in little boats, without a harbour into which he dare sail openly, even in monsoon weather.'

'I take it that your idea is that we should work together in this project?'

'Yes. I will get the rubber and you will provide the transport.'

'At the same time you could probably pick up useful information about what the Japs are doing in Burma and Malaya,' suggested the Air Commodore.

'Information reaches me constantly,' declared Li Chi.

'That should be a useful sideline,' asserted the Air Commodore. He turned to Biggles. 'Well, what do you think of the scheme?'

'I assume that you are thinking of opening a sort of ferry service between the Archipelago and India?'

'That's it—and the Higher Command is satisfied that you are the man for the job if you will take it on. How do you feel about it?'

'At first glance the scheme sounds most attractive,' said Biggles slowly. 'But when you examine it from the technical angle it doesn't look so good.'

'You mean, being so near the enemy?'

Biggles made a slight gesture of disdain. 'I wasn't even thinking of that. I was thinking of moving five thousand tons of dead weight across twelve hundred miles of ocean. If we tackle it, it will be the biggest air transportation job ever undertaken. The biggest air-craft built is a cockleshell compared with a ship. Ship-masters think in terms of hundreds of tons. Pilots think in pounds and hundredweights. There isn't an airfield, or even an emergency landing ground, in the islands, which means that the work will have to be done by marine aircraft.'

'Why not?' put in Li Chi anxiously. 'I was thinking of flying boats. They are big.'

'Yes, I'll own they're big, so big that most of the useful load is taken up by their own weight. They do fine for mails and first class passengers, but five thousand tons of merchandise is another matter. It would be like trying to move a mountain with a spade and bucket. We should be on the job for the duration.'

'Not necessarily. Or at least, I don't see why you should,' remarked the Air Commodore.

'Of course, it depends on how the thing is tackled,' admitted Biggles. 'Obviously, the greater the number of machines employed, the sooner the job would be done; but are you prepared to detail an armada for transport work? Even if you did. . . .'

'Go on.'

'All right. As I see it there are two ways of doing the operation. One: you could use a small number of machines. That would mean a long job, but the operation might pass unnoticed by the enemy. Call that the slow but sure method. Two: by putting on a big fleet of aircraft you might carry the thing through at a rush. I know that sounds attractive, but consider the snags. In the first place it would mean an imposing concentration of big machines at the nearest convenient marine aircraft establishment. The existence of such a concentration would soon be known to the enemy — you can't hope to keep a hundred flying boats under a hat. This air fleet would be watched by enemy

23

reconnaissance machines. When it took off it would be intercepted and attacked. To carry any weight worth talking about, these machines would have to be stripped of most of their armament. They wouldn't be able to fight back. A fighter escort for a round trip of over two thousand miles is out of the question. It doesn't need much imagination to see what might happen. If enemy fighters came along, this beautiful armada would be in the position of a flock of sheep attacked by a pack of wolves. We might lose the lot. Not only would we lose valuable machines and personnel, but the rubber, too. And there is another point to consider. Li Chi says he can carry on collecting rubber—from this fellow Marling for example. A small number of machines operating one at a time—by night perhaps—might escape observation for months. An air fleet could not hope to do that. I'm not trying to be awkward, but that's how I see it.'

'You are in favour of using a small number of machines—a well-knit, highly mobile force?'

'Definitely.'

'Well, and why not?'

'The big thing against it is the time factor. Let's get down to brass tacks. To give you an idea of what we are taking on, let us suppose for a moment that an airfield for land planes could be found on one of the islands. The best weight carrier is probably the Liberator 32,* such as is used by the Atlantic Ferry. It's practically a service Liberator stripped of military

---

* American-built by Consolidated, converted from the four-engined heavy bomber which carried a maximum bomb load of 12800lb, armed with nine machine guns for defence.

equipment. The Liberator can carry a disposable load of around twenty-two thousand pounds—say ten tons. With five machines operating we could carry fifty tons per trip. Fifty into five thousand goes a hundred times. In other words, it means that five Liberators would have to make a hundred trips to get the stuff across. That's using *land planes*. Imagine what it will be like with marine aircraft, which can't lift anything like that load. As a commercial proposition it would be fantastic—'

'It isn't a commercial proposition,' broke in the Air Commodore. 'Money doesn't matter. Rubber does.'

'So what? Using flying boats we should grow old getting the stuff across.'

'You talk of using five machines. Why only five?'

'Because I've only enough pilots in my squadron to operate that number. Except on rare occasions two pilots would be needed for each machine, to take turn and turn about at the stick. Even so it would be hard work. If only there was some way of using land planes the job might be done in half the time.'

'Would it be possible to make a landing ground?'

Biggles shook his head. 'From what I remember of the islands—not a hope. They are mostly hills, and covered with virgin jungle into the bargain. Still, I could have a look round. In fact, the only sensible way to start on a job of this size would be to make a survey.' Biggles turned again to Li Chi, whose expression was now one of disappointment. 'What had you in mind for a landing ground?'

'I was thinking of flying boats.'

'Yes, I know. But you must have had an idea about the best spot to use?'

'I thought the big lake on Elephant Island. It is sheltered in bad weather, and being surrounded by jungle, would not be easy to see from above. That is why I have used Elephant Island as a base to store the rubber.'

'I know the place. It has much to recommend it,' agreed Biggles. 'We could use it as our base while making a survey—I shall use a flying boat for that purpose of course.' Biggles turned back to the Air Commodore. 'I think that's about as far as we can get until I've had a look round.'

'All right. I'm content to leave the thing in your hands. Make your own arrangements. You can have anything you need in the way of equipment.'

Biggles spoke to his Chinese ally. 'Is it your intention to return to the islands as you came, or will you fly with me and act as guide?'

'I will fly with you,' answered Li Chi without hesitation.

'Good. In that case we'll see about getting things fixed up. How much flying have you done?'

'One trip—the one I made with you. Doubtless you remember it?'

Biggles grinned. 'I'm not likely to forget it.'

Li Chi smiled. 'Often, since, I have wished for wings.'

'I'll bet you have,' murmured Biggles slyly. 'It looks as if your wish is coming true. Where are you staying?'

'The Savoy Hotel.'

Biggles rose. 'All right, then.' To the Air Commodore he said: 'I'll think this over, sir, and let you have my proposals within twenty-four hours.'

'Fine. Remember, the rubber is all that matters. Everything else is secondary.'

Biggles saluted, nodded to Li Chi, who bowed gravely, and returned to the airfield. He arrived just before lunch and went straight to the ante-room, where he found the officers of the squadron assembled, anticipating his return. All eyes asked a question, but his senior flight commander, Algy Lacey, put it direct.

'I imagine the Air House has had another rush of blood to the brain?' he observed. 'What dizzy scheme have they thought of now?'

'Not dizzy—say interesting.'

'Where are we going?'

'Mergui Archipelago—Lower Burma, and possibly Malaya,' answered Biggles briefly.

Algy frowned. 'But that territory is occupied by the Japanese.'

Biggles smiled. 'So I'm told. That's why it should be interesting.'

'And just what are we going to do when we get there?' inquired Ginger suspiciously.

'As far as I can make out we're going to set up a sort of shop,' returned Biggles lightly. 'If all goes well it should develop into quite an emporium.'

'What are we going to deal in—coconuts?'

'No. We're going to be rubber merchants in a big way.'

'Hot water bottles, by Jove, and all that sort of thing,' murmured Bertie Lissie.

'If there's one thing you won't want in Burma old lad, it's a hot water bottle,' declared Biggles amid laughter. 'Let's go into lunch. We've work to do.'

# Chapter 3
# Sortie to Elephant Island

A fortnight after the conference at the Air Ministry, Biggles was over the Mergui Archipelago in a Gosling aircraft, a twin-engined, general-utility amphibian, specially fitted for the flight with long-range tanks.* Biggles had chosen this type from the small number of amphibious machines available because it suited his purpose admirably. The accommodation was right. The comparatively slow cruising speed was an advantage for survey work, and a slow landing speed was desirable in view of the nature of the mission, which would call for landings on unknown waters. For this same reason, with the ever-present risk of the keel being torn by rock or coral, a hull with watertight compartments was to be preferred to one of orthodox design, which would become waterlogged and probably sink if it came into collision with an obstruction.

Beside him in the cockpit sat Li Chi. Behind were Algy, Ginger and Bertie; apart from watching for hostile aircraft they had no particular duties, radio silence for obvious reasons being strictly observed; but Biggles was anxious that they should get a clear picture of the

* This machine, an American built high-wing cantilever all-metal monoplane, carries the U.S. Navy and Coastguard designation of J4F-1 but in the R.A.F. it is known as the Gosling. The hull is divided into five watertight compartments. There is enclosed seating accommodation for five passengers. Cruising speed is about 150 m.p.h. See cover illustration

scene of operations. He had set a course to strike the northern end of the archipelago; then, turning south, he had flown down the chain of islands looking for a possible landing ground. That there was none did not surprise him, for he could not recall from memory any island with a level area large enough to permit the landing of heavy aircraft, even if the ground were cleared. Almost without exception the islands were hilly and densely wooded, so, turning at the southern extremity, he headed back for Elephant Island, where Li Chi's headquarters had been established, and where a landing on the central lake—an area of water nearly two miles long by a quarter of a mile wide—presented no apparent difficulty. The other members of the squadron were waiting in India for instructions that would be forthcoming as a result of the reconnaissance.

From five thousand feet the seascape presented a fascinating picture, although this meant little to Biggles, to whom such scenes were no novelty. To the left lay the intense blue of the Indian Ocean rolling away and away to fade at last in the pitiless distance. To the right, the horizon was defined by a long dark stain that was the forest-clad hinterland of Lower Burma. Below the aircraft, like a string of green beads dropped carelessly on blue velvet, were the islands of the archipelago, lonely, untouched by civilization, each hiding beneath its tangle of jungle a wealth of animal, bird and reptile life, which a stranger to the tropics would not from a distance have suspected. But Biggles knew; so did Algy and Ginger, for they were not without experience of the region.* They knew that among

* See *Biggles and the Secret Mission* published by Red Fox

other things the forests provided a secure retreat for elephants, tigers, rhinoceroses, panthers, wild pigs, crocodiles, snakes of many kinds—including the venomous cobra and the huge python—and insects in countless myriads; fever-carrying mosquitoes and sand-flies being perhaps the most to be feared. Against the minute but vicious sandfly, which regards a mosquito net as no obstacle to its advance, there is no defence. In the turquoise water that separated the islands from the mainland, seeming from above so innocent of danger, lurked marine monsters of unbelievable size and horror—shark, octopus and the giant decapod.

Over Elephant Island, after a scrutiny of the surrounding atmosphere, Biggles throttled back and made a safe landing on the lake, afterwards taxying on to a point indicated by Li Chi. But as the machine surged on his eyes turned more and more to the banks, and at the end he allowed the aircraft to run to a stop well clear of the shore-line.

'Who are all these people?' he demanded sharply. There was no need for him to qualify the word people, for a number of men were congregating with excited gestures to meet the unusual visitor.

'Fear nothing,' answered Li Chi. 'They all work for me, at one thing or another.'

But the furrow in Biggles' brow did not clear. 'What's happened here? This place is altogether different from when I last saw it.'

'To what do you refer?' asked Li Chi complacently.

'The timber, for one thing. It looks as if someone has been cutting down the trees. And what about that building over there?' Biggles pointed.

'The work was done by the timber company,' said Li Chi.

'Timber company! What timber company? You didn't say anything to me about a timber company.'

'It seemed of no importance.'

'Well, this is a lot different from what I expected,' stated Biggles tersely. 'The place looks occupied— almost civilized. What's happened?'

While this conversation had been going on the others had come forward.

'What's going on here?' asked Algy. 'The place looks like the establishment of a teak-wallah.'*

'That's just what I was saying,' asserted Biggles.

Li Chi held up his hands, palms upwards, to explain. 'It *was* the establishment of teak-wallahs,' said he. 'Perhaps I should have told you. If I did not it was because I attached no importance to it. This is what happened. About a year before the war a British-Indian company obtained a concession from the government to exploit the timber which abounds on the islands. They established themselves here and began work on the nearest trees, cutting down a great number, as you can see.' He pointed. 'There is the sawmill. It was erected shortly before the war broke out. Japan's entry into the war, and the occupation of Burma and Malaya, put a stop to everything. The white men sailed away—it was all they could do to save their lives. Now you understand why all these teak logs have been left lying on the banks.'

'Why were they not sawn up?' asked Algy.

'To do that it would have been necessary to float

* Slang: man who grows and trades in teak

31

them to the mill, and for six months after being cut teak will not float on water.'

'But the sawmill is still working!' exclaimed Biggles.

Li Chi smiled. 'Why not? This is how I found things when I came here. It seemed a pity to waste all this good material. When the war is over I shall need a new junk, so I set the men to work sawing the logs into planks in readiness for building. In fact, work on my new junk has already begun.'

'What men are these?' asked Biggles.

'The men who were here; the workmen employed by the company; Chinese, Malays, Burmese, Tamil and Dyak labourers; they had nowhere to go; had they gone to the mainland the Japanese would have made slaves of them. So they stayed here, hiding in the jungle-covered hills, where they were comparatively safe. At least they were free. Most of these men were skilled in the timber trade, fellers or sawyers, so I decided to keep them busy. I pay them of course. In addition they share the comforts of my old crew and receive medical attention from me—a matter of some importance in a country where sickness and accident are the rule rather than the exception.'

'A useful arrangement,' agreed Biggles. He was looking at the men, and the timber, with a pensive look in his eyes. 'I'm just wondering if they couldn't be more usefully employed than in building a junk. By thunder! I believe it could be done.'

'What could be done?' asked Ginger.

Biggles's manner became enthusiastic. He seemed to be amused, too, and the others, who knew this mood, prepared themselves for something unusual. They were not disappointed.

'I think we could adapt this lake as an airfield for land planes,' announced Biggles.

'Here, I say old boy, you must have had the sun on the back of your neck while we were tootling across that beastly ocean—if you see what I mean?' asserted Bertie.

'Nothing like it,' returned Biggles warmly. 'This lake is the only flat patch in the islands. Yes, I know it's wet but it needn't stay that way. With thousands of teak logs weighing a ton apiece, and unlimited labour, what more do we want? Imagine all these logs floating on the water. They would provide a foundation steady enough to carry a brigade of tanks. All we have to do is to cover them with smooth planking and we have a landing deck. Li Chi says he has been sawing planks. We could make a runway even if we didn't cover the entire lake.'

'I say, by Jove, that's an idea,' declared Bertie, adjusting his eyeglass better to survey the scene. 'Make a bally aircraft carrier of the place—what?'

'That's it,' agreed Biggles. 'An aircraft carrier with a landing deck several times larger than any ship that ever put to sea.'

'I hate sloshing cold water on your brainwave, but how long do you suppose it will be before the Japs spot this beautiful contrivance?' inquired Algy, a trifle cynically.

'I don't agree that they need see it,' returned Biggles promptly. 'The water is dark blue, seen from the air. What's to stop us having a deck the same colour? The Japs don't come here, although they may fly over. Put yourself in the position of a pilot. Would you, looking down on what you knew had always been a sheet of water, suppose that it had suddenly developed a solid surface?'

'No,' admitted Algy.

'There's another angle to that,' went on Biggles. 'If for any reason a Japanese aircraft did decide to land here, it would certainly not be a land plane. It would be a marine aircraft. It doesn't need much imagination to visualize the result.'

'What fun—what fun,' murmured Bertie. 'All my life I have wondered what would happen if a flying boat had to touch down on jolly old terra firma.'

'This may be your chance to find out,' answered Biggles smiling.

'I should like to be close enough to see the pilot's face when his keel hit the deck,' said Ginger.

'Here, I say, that's a bit much old boy,' protested Bertie.

'There would be nothing to prevent enemy machines from spotting our planes, when they were here,' argued Algy.

'Oh yes, there would,' replied Biggles. 'We could build rough sheds at one end of the runway and camouflage them with branches—and there'll be plenty of branches to spare when we start shifting the timber. Dash it, we could make our sheds look so much like an extension of the forest that the birds wouldn't know the difference.'

There was silence for a minute, as if everyone was pondering on the scheme.

'What do *you* think of it, Li Chi?' inquired Biggles.

'I am amazed,' said Li Chi. 'I should never have thought of it. More and more I begin to understand why you British succeed. You have an answer for everything. It is the simplicity of the project that overcomes me.'

'Will the labourers be all right?'

'This will so much tickle their sense of humour that they will work twenty hours a day,' returned Li Chi. 'Without pay, and without going on strike,' he added slyly.

'How long will it take to do the job?'

'By using the logs near the water, and the planks already cut, a temporary runway could be made in a few hours. We shall need a lot of nails, though—a lot more than I have here.'

'We can soon fetch some nails—with the paint and brushes.'

'Then I will give orders for the work to start this moment,' declared Li Chi.

'Oh no—not so fast,' objected Biggles. 'You can get the logs rolled down to the water if you like, but you mustn't start the planking till we get the paint. The art of camouflage is to do it as you go. Suppose an enemy reconnaissance pilot were to fly over tomorrow, and again in a few days? He might not realize what was going on, but he would see a difference—and in modern warfare any change in the scenery invites suspicion. Suspicion is followed by investigation. We must paint as we go, and we shall have to have scouts out to watch for the approach of enemy aircraft. If that happens everyone will have to take cover.'

'I understand,' acknowledged Li Chi. 'I suggest we build the runway first, and then go on working until the whole lake is covered.'

'That's the idea,' answered Biggles. 'The first things we need are paint, brushes and nails. I think I had

35

better stay here to plan the details. Algy, after you've had a spot of lunch you'll take the Gosling back to India to get the necessary equipment. We shall need a deuce of a lot of paint—get all the stuff you can lay hands on. Get in touch with Raymond and tell him I've decided to use land planes. We'll start with five. The gang can bring them across. I should also like a couple of long-range fighters for defence, or for escort work, should it become necessary. I suggest a couple of Lightnings.* They have some in the reserve pool at Delhi.'

'Lightnings will arrive here with empty tanks,' Algy pointed out.

'Yes, but as soon as we get the thing going we can lay in a store of oil and petrol. The Liberators might as well fly loaded both ways. They can bring fuel and stores out and take rubber back. As you will be flying lightly loaded you can bring more petrol back with you. Don't waste time—get back. Things are liable to happen quickly on a show like this. Bertie can go with you for company. Ginger had better stay here with me.'

'The squadron is going to be busy if it is to operate five transports and two fighters,' observed Algy dubiously.

'The fellows can take turn and turn about flying the Liberators,' answered Biggles. 'With two pilots standing by the fighters, we shall always have two resting. I don't suppose there will be much for the fighters to

---

* American Lockheed Lightning, a twin-engined single seat fighter armed with a cannon and four machine guns. Top speed 350 mph.

do—at least I hope not. All right. Let's go ashore and rip the lid off a can of bully.'*

* Slang: corned beef

# Chapter 4
# Ginger Takes a Walk

The party went ashore under the curious eyes of as motley a collection of humanity as Ginger could remember seeing anywhere. They were not a pretty lot to look at, either, he decided, although in this respect the conditions in which they were living were no doubt largely responsible. Clothing was skimpy, threadbare and dirty, as was to be expected. The most popular garment was the *sarong*, the shirt-like dress worn by the working class throughout the Isthmus of Malaya. One or two Chinese had blue dungaree trousers. Every man carried a weapon of some sort, if only a knife. Firearms were rare, and of obsolete pattern; but the *parang*, the heavy curved sword of the district, was common.

One man stood out in ugliness and ferociousness of appearance—a tall, gaunt Malay, minus one eye, and a face so scarred that Ginger shuddered when he looked at it. His expression, due to the scars, was demoniacal, and not improved by a dirty red handkerchief tied low over his forehead. From a wide belt, exquisitely decorated with gold, silver and mother-of-pearl, hung a huge *parang*. Thrust into a sash were a knife and a modern service revolver. The sinister appearance of this musical comedy bandit was rendered almost ludicrous by an enormous, obviously home-made cigar. As a final touch the man walked with a pronounced limp.

Li Chi introduced him as Ayert, his bosun, observing

in a low voice that the facial distortion was the result of an affair with a tiger, and the limp, the outcome of an argument with a crocodile when he was a boy. Nevertheless, asserted Li Chi, Ayert was the finest sailing master from the Indian Ocean to the China Sea, a man renowned for daring and courage even in that race of tough fighters, the Malays. 'Pay no attention to his looks,' concluded Li Chi. 'Ayert is tough. He fears nothing that walks, crawls or swims. Upon his loyalty you may depend. Be careful of how you speak of him, for he is proud, and from long association with me at Indian ports, speaks a fair amount of English.'

The subject of this conversation approached and spoke volubly for two or three minutes to his Boss in a language unknown to the others. When he had finished Li Chi turned to Biggles with one of those faint, subtle smiles that they were beginning to know.

'Ayert has just given me interesting news,' he said smoothly. 'Ten miles away, on the mainland, has come a man, a Japanese, who is not only my greatest enemy, but would give his arms to catch me alive. Perhaps that is why he has come here; or it may be that his government has sent him here because he knows the islands. He is in complete control of the district and has set up his headquarters at Victoria Point, the nearest village across the strait.'

'Who is this chap?' asked Biggles.

'Admiral Tamashoa,' was the answer. 'Before the war he was the owner of the biggest pearling fleet in these waters. His divers found many fine pearls, but they did not all reach Tamashoa.'

'Why not?'

'Because I was pearling in the same waters and it

seemed a pity to let such lovely things go to such a beast,' said Li Chi smoothly. 'He treated his Malay divers abominably, forcing them to dive in such deep water that their lungs burst. Because he knew where his best pearls were going he became very angry with me, and uttered threats which—as I am still here—served no useful purpose.'

Biggles' eyes twinkled. 'Now I understand why they used to call you a pirate.'

Li Chi held out his hands appealingly. 'It is not piracy to take the property of a man who acquires it by brutality and murder,' he protested. 'As I made you a present of a pair of the pearls you should be glad. If I am a pirate, so, too, are you, for receiving stolen goods.'

'So *that's* where you got them,' said Biggles, affecting reproach.

'What did you do with them?'

'I sold them to buy a new aeroplane.'

'How much did you get for them?'

'Eight thousand pounds.'

Li Chi shook his head. 'There was another robber in the bargain. You were swindled. Those pearls were worth twelve thousand.'

'Well, as you got them for nothing and I got them for nothing, we've nothing to complain about,' returned Biggles, grinning.

'Tamashoa knew of those two pink pearls,' said Li Chi seriously. 'Such was his mortification when he lost them that he sent a special messenger to me offering to buy them back at any price, as he wanted them for his favourite lady. I sent word that I no longer had them. He asked me what had become of them. I told him that I had given them as a present to a British flying man named Major Bigglesworth for saving my life. No doubt he will remember the name, so it is to be hoped that he will never be in a position to ask you about the pearls, personally.'

'I'll bear it in mind,' replied Biggles thoughtfully. 'But this won't do. Let's have lunch. The sooner the Gosling is on the way back to India the better.'

'Come to my house,' invited Li Chi. 'It is not all that I would wish and my hospitality has been affected by the war, but I still live fairly comfortably, as you will see.'

He led the way into the forest, and presently a long, low bungalow, which until now the jungle had concealed, came into view. If, thought Ginger as he entered, it was not all that the owner could wish, then Li Chi must be a man of fastidious taste, for judged by western standards the appointments were luxurious, although, of course, Oriental. It reminded Ginger that their host was a Chinese—a fact which, in view of his London-made clothes and correct English, it was easy to forget. But when, with a word of apology Li Chi left his guests to return a few minutes later in Chinese dress, any delusion was banished. He was at once in keeping with his surroundings.

The meal, a curious mixture of eastern and western dishes, provided by a Malay cook who had obviously been at some trouble to please his master's guests, was a cheerful affair, so much so that Ginger began to regard the enterprise in a different light. If nothing occurred to mar the tranquillity of Elephant Island, he decided, the sortie should turn out to be a pleasant interlude in the hard business of war.

41

The meal over, they all returned to the lake, and soon afterwards Algy and Bertie took off on the return trip to India for the tasks which Biggles had assigned to them. Biggles, Ginger and Li Chi watched them go, and afterwards stood talking for some time. Biggles observed that he thought it strange that Li Chi should be allowed to live so near Japanese occupied territory without interference. Li Chi asserted that the reason was evident. There were some hundreds of islands, large and small, in the archipelago, and for the Japanese to maintain a garrison on every one, as well as on the tens of thousands of other islands in the Pacific war zone, would demand more troops than even the Japanese possessed. So the enemy did the next best thing. It maintained air and sea patrols to keep watch, although the personnel employed in these duties, being in small numbers, rarely landed. Said Li Chi: 'Of course, the Japanese know there are refugees on the islands, but it would be a tremendous task to round them up, so, as it was supposed that they could do no harm, they were left alone.'

'We may alter that,' remarked Biggles. 'One day it will be the Japs, with their communications severed, who will be hiding on the islands.'

'That state of affairs will not last long,' returned Li Chi casually. 'The Malays will hunt them down and decorate their doorposts with Japanese heads. Come and look at the sawmill. We are cutting up magnificent timber.'

This suggestion made no appeal to Ginger, who, nevertheless, accompanied the others as far as the mill. But he did not enter. Instead, finding a narrow path leading uphill through the jungle, he strolled along it with the object of getting a view of the island from the eminence thus gained. As far as the jungle was concerned there was little of interest. In the shade of the great trees the air was hot and humid, and sweat was soon trickling down his face. What with this, and finding the path rather longer than he expected, he took advantage of a seat offered by a fallen tree, to rest. Once, as he sat there, he thought he heard a slight sound in the forest, but he paid little attention to it. There were, he knew, many wild creatures in the jungle, but he did not suppose that there was anything to fear so near to the lumber camp. But as the minutes passed he became aware of an extraordinary sensation of uneasiness for which he could not account, and this soon pressed upon him to such an extent that he picked up a lump of rotten wood and hurled it into the bushes. Nothing happened, and he was about to move on when suddenly he saw something that induced a prickling sensation in his spine. It was a face. At first he was by no means sure that it was a face. But it looked like a face, a man's face, staring at him, not at shoulder height as a human face would normally be, but from low down, as if the man were crouching, or even lying. Dappled sunlight falling on the spot made it difficult to see the object clearly. It did not move.

Now Ginger had Li Chi's word for it that the people on the island were friendly; and he did not forget this. Consequently he was more than a little puzzled by the occurrence, particularly as the expression on the face was positively malevolent. It was this expression that alarmed him, and at the same time fascinated him. It was horrible, hateful. Still it did not move, and that, perhaps, was the most trying part of all. Why should

43

the man—if indeed it was a man—crouch there staring at him in such a way? For this question he could find no reasonable answer. Had the man attacked him it would have been altogether different. He would have drawn the automatic he carried and, if necessary, used it. But he hardly felt justified in shooting at a man for nothing more than staring at him, or possibly trying to scare him.

This state of affairs persisted for about three minutes, although to Ginger it seemed longer. But by the end of that time he had had enough of it, and determined to end the matter one way or the other. Quite slowly he drew his pistol, and taking aim at the face, said loudly, in English: 'Come out of that.'

The result of this order exceeded anything he expected. The face disappeared. There was a crashing in the undergrowth. Running forward Ginger was just in time to see a dirty yellow *sarong*, caught in round the waist with a blue sash, disappearing into the bushes. He did not follow. For some minutes he could hear the crashing, growing ever fainter, proceeding down the hill towards the sea which here and there could be discerned through gaps in the trees. Wondering at this strange adventure he abandoned his original idea of climbing to the top of the knoll; instead he returned to the lake, to find Biggles, Li Chi and Ayert, in conversation outside the sawmill.

Biggles glanced at him casually, but then looked quickly back at him again. 'What have you been up to?' he asked, looking hard at Ginger's face.

'I've been for a stroll,' replied Ginger.

'What happened, you look pale?'

'I had a funny adventure,' said Ginger, smiling

sheepishly, for now he was back on safe ground the incident seemed trivial. 'As I walked up the hill I saw a face staring at me from the bushes. The owner of it may have been friendly, but if looks could cut a throat, he would have cut mine.'

Li Chi spoke sharply. 'Did you see this man?'

'Not exactly. All I can say is that his face seemed lighter in colour than most of those I've seen here. When I went towards him he bolted. He wore an old yellow *sarong* and blue sash.'

Li Chi looked at Ayert. Ayert looked at his master.

'You know this fellow I see?' murmured Biggles.

Li Chi drew a deep breath. 'Yes, we know him. His name is Pamboo—at least, that's what everyone calls him. Just what his nationality is I don't know, but one of his parents must have been European. That does not matter, but he is a bad character—an incorrigible. He came to me first a long time ago, asking for work. He admitted that he had been in prison at Singapore, but I cared little about that. I took him on. Later, I learned that he was, as you say, a real bad hat, a thief and a murderer. Among other exploits, while working on a rubber plantation he had killed an overseer. I began to think about this when things started to disappear. I set a trap, and we discovered that this rascal was the culprit. That was after we came here. After warning him several times, for none of my men are what you would call angels, I ordered him to be flogged—that is the way we deal with a thief in this part of the world. After the punishment was administered he feigned sickness, with the result that his guards relaxed their vigilance and he escaped into the jungle where, although a search has been made for him, he remains in hiding. If he could do us an injury he would seize the chance, although he has little hope of that here. Still, it would be a good thing if we could catch him.' Turning to Ginger, Li Chi concluded, 'Would you mind showing Ayert where you saw this rascal? He might be able to track him.'

Ginger having expressed willingness to do this they set off, leaving Biggles and Li Chi to proceed with their planning.

By the time Ginger and his companion had arrived at the spot where the incident had occurred the sun was low over the horizon, and the light was beginning to fade. However, Ayert soon picked up the fugitive's tracks, and with his drawn *parang* in his hand followed them down the hill until they were within sound of the murmur of the sea. And there, suddenly, Ayert stopped. He pointed out across the placid strait that separated the island from the mainland. 'Look, *tuan*,'* said he. 'He escapes us.'

There was no need for Ginger to ask Ayert to explain. Two miles away, a mere speck on the lonely sea, a canoe was being paddled swiftly towards the mainland.

'Can we get another boat and follow him?' queried Ginger.

Ayert held up five fingers. 'Soon—five minute—dark. No moon. No catchee.'

'In that case we may as well go home,' replied Ginger, more disturbed in his mind than he cared to admit. Pamboo had seen white men on Elephant Island. No doubt he'd seen the aircraft. He had fled to the mainland, not only to escape, but perhaps to sell

* Malay: Sir

46

his information to the Japanese. It was not difficult to predict what the result would be.

Deep in thought Ginger followed his companion through the silent jungle back to the camp.

# Chapter 5

# Biggles Makes a Reconnaissance

Biggles received Ginger's news about the escape of Pamboo with concern; Li Chi with anger.

'I do not understand how he could have got a canoe,' said Li Chi.

Ayert gave it as his opinion that the man had already been to the mainland since his escape from Li Chi's custody. He asserted that the craft in which Pamboo had fled was a *prahu*, not one of which was to be found on Elephant Island. 'How did he get it?' went on Ayert, his one good eye glaring. 'When he run away he sit along beach. Bimeby comes Salones with *kabang*. They not know he bad man. They think he Li Chi man. They sail him across strait to *kampong*. Pamboo go to Tamashoa. Tamashoa send him back in *prahu* to spy. He come. See white man. Go back now to Tamashoa.'

Li Chi explained to Biggles and Ginger that Salones were a tribe of inoffensive travellers, sea gipsies who wandered from island to island in the boats in which they lived, called *kabangs*. The *kampong* to which Ayert had referred was the local name for a village. Thus, what Ayert had meant to convey was, that Pamboo, when he had escaped, had managed to get the sea gipsies to give him a lift to the mainland, where he had reported to the Japanese commander. Tamashoa had sent him back in a *prahu*, a native canoe, to watch Li Chi's movements. 'Pamboo, by the way, is Malayan for snake,' concluded Li Chi. 'The fellow is well named.'

Biggles nodded. 'If Ayert is right it boils down to this. Tamashoa knows you are here. Very soon he will know that a British aircraft has landed here, although he won't know for what purpose.'

'I think so,' agreed Li Chi.

'Tamashoa will also have been told that the sawmill is working, cutting planks,' continued Biggles.

'True, but he will think the planks are for the purpose for which I originally intended them—to enable me to build a new junk.'

'Even so, he is not likely to let you get away with that,' averred Biggles.

Li Chi admitted that it was unlikely.

'You know the workings of the eastern mind better than we do,' alleged Biggles. 'What do you think Tamashoa will do?'

Li Chi considered the question for a moment before he answered. 'He will wait a little while to lull us into the belief that he knows nothing, hoping that our vigilance will relax. Then he will make a sudden attack, hoping to take us by surprise. He will burn the sawmill and the planks, and, if he can, take prisoners, who for his amusement he will torture to death. I fear our plan is likely to be put out of joint unless we can get the rubber away before he strikes—or, of course, unless we can think of some plan to outwit him.'

'It looks as though we shall have to do some serious thinking,' observed Biggles. 'How about moving to another island?'

'To move the rubber and the rest of my property

would require many boats which we do not possess; and even if we had them the boats would be seen by Japanese patrols.'

Biggles tapped a cigarette thoughtfully on the back of his hand. 'It seems certain that we shall not be left here in peace for very long.'

'Of that we may be sure,' agreed Li Chi imperturbably.

'Then the thing is to get the rubber away before Tamashoa comes across.'

'That is all we can do.'

'What a hope we've got,' put in Ginger. 'It will be a week before we start operating.'

'Unless. . . .'

'Unless what?'

Biggles looked at Li Chi. 'What about this Major Marling you were telling us about? You say he has rubber hidden on his plantation, which is buried away in the Burmese jungle. Instead of his rubber being brought here in small quantities wouldn't it be better if we flew direct to his plantation and collected it — that is, if we could find some sort of landing ground?'

'No doubt it would be better — if there was a landing ground.'

'What sort of country is it? Is it flat . . . open?'

'There are flat places near the river — the paddy fields, where rice is grown.'

'I feel inclined to go and have a look at this place and have a word with Major Marling,' said Biggles thoughtfully. 'It would do no harm anyway.'

'You could not fly there for there is no landing ground,' Li Chi pointed out. 'Even the river, the Pak Chan, at its headwaters, is choked with weeds, except for a narrow channel made by canoes. And the river winds very much.'

'Could we go by boat?'

'Yes. A *kabang* borrowed from the Salones could go up the river without attracting much attention or suspicion. *Kabangs* are always moving about.'

'How long would the trip take?'

'The distance from here is about sixty miles—fifty miles up the river. The outward journey, against the current, would take not less than fifteen or sixteen hours even with a fair wind to fill our sail across the strait. The return trip, travelling with the stream, could be done in less time. But I doubt if Major Marling would receive you. He is a strange man.'

'You could give me a letter of introduction.'

'It would be better if I went with you,' offered Li Chi. 'Now that I have got the men started here the work could go on without me.'

'That's fine,' declared Biggles. 'But we can't go until Algy comes back. That should be tomorrow. We must tell him what has happened, and what we propose doing about it.'

'Of course,' concurred Li Chi.

'Let's think it over,' decided Biggles. 'There's nothing more we can do at present—except that you might see about getting hold of a *kabang*.'

This Li Chi promised to do, and since darkness had put an end to outdoor activities they walked back to the bungalow for the evening meal, after which the discussion was resumed until bedtime, without any change being made in the main plan.

Dawn the following day found work on the floating airfield in full swing, every available man lending a willing hand in the task of rolling the logs down to the water, where they were lashed together with rattans, a plentiful supply of which was available in the adjacent jungle. The logs, as they were placed in position, were covered with brushwood. Biggles and Ginger supervised the erection of a covered shelter over a tiny bay to house the Gosling when it returned, and to conceal it from enemy eyes. Ayert went off to find a party of sea gipsies and arrange for the hire of their *kabang*.

Work had not been long in progress when confirmation of their suspicions, that Pamboo had gone over to the Japanese, was provided by the arrival of an enemy aircraft—a Mitsubishi naval flying boat. The noise of the engine gave warning of its approach. The natives, having received instructions from Li Chi, dropped what they were doing and vanished into the convenient jungle. The engine in the sawmill was stopped, so that by the time the aircraft was overhead not a sign of life was to be seen. With a significance which Biggles did not fail to notice, the machine flew a straight course from the mainland to Elephant Island, and, moreover, flew direct to the lake. It then made six short flights from north to south, moving a mile or two westward each time, which told the watching airmen what the pilot was doing as if he himself had made the announcement for their benefit.

'Photographic reconnaissance,' murmured Biggles, as the plane made off eastward. 'He exposed at least a dozen plates, covering the whole area. In a little while no doubt Tamashoa will be going over the pictures with a magnifying glass to ascertain if Pamboo has told the truth. I don't think he'll see very much, but this gives us fair warning to watch our step.'

As soon as the machine had disappeared from sight, work was resumed, and continued without further interruption until lunch time, when the drone of an aero engine, this time approaching from the west, caused a second stoppage. But it was brief, for looking out from cover Biggles and Ginger saw the Gosling skimming low towards the rendezvous. In a few minutes it was on the lake, taxying towards its newly erected hangar. As soon as it had been safely moored Algy and Bertie got out to report an uneventful trip. They had brought paint, brushes and nails, all that were immediately available. Further supplies were being collected, reported Algy, and could be fetched the following day. What they had brought would do to be going on with.

The work of unloading was put in hand.

Later, in the bungalow, Algy made a more detailed report. He had been in touch with Air Commodore Raymond through service radio, with the result that the remainder of the squadron would assemble with five Liberators and two Lightnings, at Madras, and there await orders to proceed to Elephant Island. In fact, Biggles' instructions had been carried out to the letter. There had been no difficulty, no hitch.

'I told the boys that it was unlikely they would be wanted here inside a week,' stated Algy.

'I'm not so sure about that,' answered Biggles, and after relating what had happened during the Gosling's absence, announced his intention of visiting Major Marling, taking Ginger and Li Chi with him. 'You can either stay here with Bertie till we get back, or better still, make another trip across to Madras to fetch a load of stuff.'

Algy agreed.

Soon afterwards Ayert came in to say that he had found a *kabang*, owned by a family of Salones, of whom two men were willing to make the trip up the Pak Chan river. It would be better to wait for darkness though, before starting, in case the *kabang* was seen leaving the island by a Japanese patrol, which might result in the craft being intercepted and examined.

To this precaution Biggles readily agreed. It did not prevent them from making the necessary preparations.

These, which consisted chiefly of victualling the craft for the voyage, were soon made by the useful Ayert who, at Li Chi's special request, was included in the party.

'As there will be plenty of room, and Ayert is an invaluable fellow to have on an adventure of this sort, I strongly advise that we take him,' said Li Chi. And so it was agreed.

'What about weapons?' asked Biggles. 'I'll take your advice on that, too.'

Li Chi reflected. 'I always travel light. We have our pistols. To be on the safe side perhaps we ought to take rifles. They would occupy little room.'

After that there was nothing to do but wait for darkness. When the hour for departure came Ayert led the way through the forest to the seashore, where, in a little cove, the Salones were waiting. It was the first time Ginger had seen the boat they were to use, and the sight of it made him wonder if he would have not done better to offer his place to Algy or Bertie. The *kabang* was in charge of two men and a small boy. One—as it was presently revealed—navigated the boat, using a long oar to steer, while the other manipulated

54

a make-shift sail. Having hauled it to the masthead he sat in the stern with the mainsheet wound round his big toe. The boy, it turned out, was merely a human pump. His job was to bale out the water that trickled constantly through warped and rotten timbers. The Salones, Ayert had told Ginger, lived almost entirely on fish, their store of this commodity being kept in the bottom of the boat; and as fish in the tropics quickly becomes 'ripe', the smell of the bilge, when it was stirred up by the boy, nearly made Ginger sick. A roof of split bamboo and dilapidated canvas walls provided protection against the sun in day-time. Accommodation was simple. The passengers merely sat on a bamboo floor just far enough above the keel to keep them out of the slush. The *kabang* was, in fact, as Ginger now discovered, a houseboat, of design and manufacture as primitive as could be imagined. Considered as a conveyance it was at the opposite end of the scale from a modern flying boat. However, the passengers were in no case to be particular, so they took their places and waved good-bye to those ashore. At a word of command from Ayert one of the Salones pushed off with his oar, and the crazy craft crept out across the darkened strait.

# Chapter 6
# Up the River

Dawn found the *kabang* far up the Pak Chan river, the sullen waterway that forms the boundary between Lower Burma and Siam,* although as both countries were occupied by the enemy there was nothing to choose between them; both were hostile. Ginger, who had dozed, awoke to find that the boat was being poled by the two Salones through comparatively shallow water, near a bank fringed by tall reeds beyond which towered the sombre tropic forest. The boy was still baling with a movement that had become automatic. A thin mist coiling and curling like steam over the surface of the winding river did nothing to enliven a scene that at best could only be described as dismal. The humid air was redolent with strange smells; predominating was the reek of river mud and rotting vegetables. Outside the boat the only movement was a V-shaped ripple that moved swiftly across the water a short distance ahead.

'*Boya*,' grunted the boy, observing that Ginger had noticed the ripple.

'Crocodile,' translated Li Chi in a low voice. 'The river is full of the beasts.'

Squatting on the bamboo floor, wearing a short kimono of yellow silk, into the wide sleeves of which

* Now Thailand

56

his hands were thrust, he was now the complete Oriental, and Ginger found it hard to believe that this was the same man who, in London, had been so correctly dressed in western style.

A chuckle took Ginger's eyes to Ayert, who was reclining in the stern. At first Ginger could not make out what he was doing. Then to his utter and complete amazement he saw that he was looking at a magazine. It was the title of the magazine that made Ginger's eyes go round with wonder. It was a film paper.

'For the love of Pete,' he murmured, turning an astonished face to Li Chi. 'Where did he get that?'

'He bought it.'

'*Bought* it—where?'

'When we were in India. He has a stack of them.' Li Chi smiled. 'Didn't you know that Ayert was a film fan?'

'A *film* fan!' Ginger was incredulous. 'Do you mean he *goes* to films?'

'On every possible occasion. In fact, before the war it was no uncommon thing for him to go hundreds of miles out of his way to visit a picture palace at Calcutta, Singapore, Penang, Renong, Rangoon—or any place within reach. He adores the films.'

Ginger blinked. 'Ayert at the flicks—that's a knockout. It's a picture I can't visualize. Can he actually read that paper he's looking at?'

'No, he can't read English, but he loves to look at the pictures. He recognises the actors and actresses. Indeed, he knows all the stars by name.'

'Who's his favourite?'

'Ask him.'

Ginger spoke to Ayert. 'Who's your favourite actor?' he asked.

'Donald Duck,' returned Ayert without hesitation. 'Very clever wise guy.'

Ginger looked at Biggles. 'That beats cock fighting.'

'In the thriller section he prefers westerns,' volunteered Li Chi. 'I make him leave his pistol with the cloakroom attendant, otherwise he's liable to take part in the shooting.'

Ginger smiled. 'I'd like to go with him some time. It should be fun.'

Biggles broke in. 'You're liable to get all the fun you want before this show is over. How much farther have we to go, Li Chi?'

'As you could fly in an aeroplane the distance to the Major's bungalow is not more than eight miles; but as the river wanders we must travel twenty miles,' was the reply. 'We're fortunate. Evidently there has been no rain at the headwaters of the river, so the current is slight. We have made good time.'

'If it is only eight miles overland to the bungalow would it not be quicker to park the boat and walk?' suggested Ginger.

Li Chi smiled. 'No, it would not be quicker. The ground is a bog and the jungle is thick. Also, there are many leeches, and other creatures which it is well to avoid. In such country as this it is more comfortable to travel by the river.'

Biscuits were produced from the food bag. Ginger munched his ration moodily, watching the banks glide past with monotonous repetition. At each bend the same view was presented. Apart from an occasional bird, or the swirl of a crocodile sliding into the water, there was nothing of interest, nothing to attract the eye. An hour passed with hardly a word spoken. Then one of the Salones rested in a listening attitude. He said nothing. His expression did not change. The man who held the steering oar looked back down the river.

'They hear something,' said Li Chi quietly.

Presently they all heard it—the distant chug-chug of an engine.

Li Chi spoke to one of the Salones in his own language. The man answered briefly. Li Chi switched his glance to Biggles. 'A patrol boat is coming up the river,' he announced. 'The men, who are quick to recognize sounds, say it is the *Lotus*, a launch of about fifty tons with a shallow draft for river work. It was once owned by a trading company, but it is now, of course, in Japanese hands.'

'What do you make of it?' asked Biggles.

'It may be merely on a routine patrol, although why the Japanese should patrol this river, where there is hardly a *kampong*, is hard to understand,' answered Li Chi thoughtfully. 'It may be that our passage has been reported by a spy, and they are following us to find out what a *kabang* is doing so far up the river. The alternative is that the launch is making for Shansie, the Major's estate. There is nowhere else for it to go. I hope it is not.'

'That would be awkward.'

'Awkward for us, but probably worse for Major Marling.'

'What had we better do about it?'

'For the moment there is only one thing we can do. The launch will quickly overtake us; we must not be seen, so obviously we must hide.' Li Chi spoke quickly to the Salones who, clearly, understood the danger. One man took the pole and put his weight on it, while the other, leaning on the oar, turned the boat towards the reeds. He then ran forward, and parting the weeds with his hands enabled the boat to enter in such a way that it left practically no sign. It came to rest with a thick screen of reeds between it and the river.

'Quiet, please, now,' said Li Chi in a low voice. 'Sound travels far over smooth water.'

Biggles dropped his cigarette into the ooze. Silence fell. The only sound was the throb of the screw of the approaching river craft. Minutes passed, with the launch drawing ever nearer, but it seemed a long time before it entered the stretch where the *kabang* had taken cover. Voices could then be heard. Ayert, regardless of the foul mud that came nearly to his waist, stepped overboard and made his way cautiously forward through the reeds until only a thin screen remained between him and the river, a position in which he remained while the launch passed. The others saw nothing. As the sounds began to recede Ayert came back, and with significant gestures whispered something to Li Chi, who allowed a little while to elapse before he translated. It turned out that the gist of Ayert's report was this: the Salones had been right. It was the *Lotus*, manned by a Japanese crew. There were about eighteen or twenty soldiers on board, with an officer. The launch was proceeding at full speed as if on a definite errand. 'It was not looking for us, though,' asserted Li Chi.

'How do you know that?' asked Biggles.

'Because had it been in pursuit of anyone, watchers would have been posted. The soldiers, Ayert says, were

60

lounging on the deck, which suggests that the vessel is still some way from its objective. It must be going to Shansie—there is nowhere else. I'm afraid something has happened to send it there at such short notice. Had the trip been a routine affair it would have been arranged some days ago, in which case I should have heard of it through my spies. Only yesterday one of my men came to me from Victoria Point and there was no talk then of a visit to Shansie. I confess this unexpected development alarms me—not for myself, but for Major Marling.'

'Has he anything to fear?' inquired Biggles.

Li Chi shrugged. 'We don't know, but it is not unlikely. If the major is taken by surprise, and the place searched before certain things can be hidden, it will be bad for him—bad for everyone at Shansie. I don't like this. I have an uneasy feeling that the major has been betrayed by a spy.'

'Did that fellow Pamboo know of your association with Major Marling?'

'I could not say for certain,' answered Li Chi slowly. 'It is possible. Some of my men know. They were bound to know. Pamboo may have heard them talking amongst themselves. One thing is certain. The major must be warned of the approach of the launch.'

'How? We can't overtake it.'

'Ayert will have to go on, travel direct overland. It is the only way.'

'Let us all go.'

'No. Alone, Ayert, who knows the jungle, will travel fast. We should only be a hindrance. Wait, please, while I speak to him.' Li Chi addressed the Malay in his native tongue. Ayert answered with a single word, whereupon the Salones, who had been listening, thrust the *kabang* out of the reeds and soon had it moving towards the opposite bank. As soon as the boat touched the side, Ayert sprang ashore, and without a backward glance plunged into the jungle.

Ginger could see no path, no track. 'Will he be able to find his way through that maze?' he asked.

'A panther needs no signposts,' returned Li Chi scornfully. A sharp word to the Salones and the *kabang* proceeded on its way up the river. 'Ayert will know where to find us when he has accomplished his mission,' stated Li Chi confidently, as he resumed his seat on the bamboo floor. 'And there is no fear of our meeting the *Lotus* coming back, for we shall hear it long before it comes into sight,' he added.

For about an hour no one spoke. Then Biggles remarked, 'Are we going right up to the estate in this boat?'

'Practically,' replied Li Chi. 'When we get so near that it would be incautious to stay on the open river we will go ashore and proceed on foot to a point where Ayert will come to us and report what is happening. If the alarm turns out to be a false one, and the *Lotus* returns down the river, we will go forward to the major as if nothing had happened.'

'But surely the Japanese will recognize him for an Englishman?' put in Ginger.

'That will depend largely on how he is dressed,' averred Li Chi. 'He has lived so long among the locals that he might easily pass for one if he so wished. But sometimes he has things lying about—English books, for instance—which would betray him, if he is not warned in time to hide them. The last time I was there

I saw such things—a violin which his son had been playing; I told him then that he should be more careful, but he seemed to think there was no risk of the Japanese coming so far up the river. You must understand that he rules like a king, and it is not easy to advise a king without giving offence. I told you that he can be a difficult man. And,' added Li Chi as an afterthought, 'his son can be a difficult fellow, too. He has courage, but also the pride of a prince—as perhaps you will see.'

Again silence fell. No sound came to indicate what was happening on the river or in the jungle. The Salones, conscious that the expedition had become urgent, laboured in heat that became more sultry as the sun climbed towards its zenith. Sweat glistened on their brown bodies. For nearly two hours the *kabang* forged on through the sluggish current, and then, rounding a bend, Li Chi spoke tersely. The Salones responded by turning from the main stream into a narrow backwater almost choked by water lilies. Up this they proceeded, not without difficulty, for some fifty yards, when the backwater broadened out and ended in a stagnant pool about the size of a tennis court. Evidently it had been used previously for the same purpose, for at the far end there was the mouldering remains of a landing stage. Behind it, a track, much overgrown, gaped like the mouth of a tunnel in liana-festooned casuarina trees. There was also a narrow mossy path round the pool.

'Ayert will find us here,' said Li Chi, rising. 'This is where, years ago, Major Marling kept his boat. We are about a quarter of a mile from the bungalow, but less from the cultivated land which surrounds it.'

'The *Lotus* must have been here for some time,' remarked Biggles.

'Not so long as you might think, because, before approaching the bungalow, the river makes a big sweep,' answered Li Chi. 'As I expected, the Japanese did not know of this short cut.'

'What had we better do?' queried Biggles. 'Shall we have a scout round or wait here for Ayert to come?'

'I think we had better wait,' decided Li Chi.

The words had hardly left his lips when from some distance ahead came a sharp fusillade of rifle shots. There were shouts, a few more sporadic shots, and again, silence.

Biggles looked at Li Chi. 'I don't like the sound of that,' he said in a tense voice.

'Nor I. I'm afraid there is trouble,' muttered Li Chi anxiously.

From no great distance came the patter of footsteps, swift with the desperate urgency of a man running for his life. Branches crackled. Twigs swished as they were flung aside. Biggles drew his pistol, and jumping ashore took up a position behind a tree. Ginger did the same. The Salones crouched in their boat, knives in their hands.

With a final spurt the runner crashed into the clearing. It was Ayert. He was panting through lips that were drawn back showing the teeth: his manner was as savage as that of a tiger brought to bay. Seeing the others, who now stepped out from cover, he came to a skidding stop, and addressing his master, broke into furious speech.

Li Chi listened with the impassive calm of his race until Ayert had finished—or until he had to stop to draw breath. Then he turned to Biggles. 'It is worse than we feared,' he said quietly. 'Much worse.'

'What's happened?' asked Biggles shortly.

'As I supposed, the Japanese objective was the bungalow at Shansie. They burst in upon Major Marling, giving him no time to hide things which he could have put away had he known the Japanese were coming. He has been arrested.'

'But I thought the object of Ayert going ahead was to warn him?'

'It was. Unfortunately some of the Japanese also disembarked higher up the river, and by marching overland, forestalled him. They marched along a track, which compelled Ayert to keep in the jungle. He was just too late to be of any use.'

'How does he know what happened at the bungalow?'

'Prince Lalla escaped and told him. They attempted a rescue. It failed. They were shot at, and were compelled to retire. In the confusion that followed they became parted.'

'Where is Prince Lalla now?'

'In the jungle somewhere, presumably hiding. Ayert, of course, made for this spot, to warn us.'

'Are the Japanese still at the bungalow?'

'They were still there a few minutes ago. If I know anything about them they will remain there, eating and drinking until there is nothing left, making a search of the whole place an excuse for staying.'

'What about the major? Where is he?'

'They were about to question him when Ayert and Prince Lalla attempted the rescue.'

'What will they do if he refuses to speak?'

'No doubt they will torture him. Be sure they will do their utmost to make him incriminate himself.'

'We can't allow that,' decided Biggles quickly.

'Can we prevent it?'

'We can try.'

'Very well,' agreed Li Chi imperturbably. 'What do you suggest?'

'You know the layout of the bungalow and its immediate surroundings, I assume?'

'Yes.'

Biggles took out his notebook. 'Make a rough sketch map of the place for me.'

'Certainly.' Li Chi took the pencil, worked rapidly for a minute and handed back the result.

# Chapter 7
# War Comes to Shansie

It was not long before certain noises ahead made it clear that the objective was at hand. Surprisingly, thought Ginger, they were those of revelry and merriment.

'Sounds as if the Japanese have found some booze,' he opined in a low voice.

'Maybe you're right,' murmured Biggles. 'But don't forget that they often laugh at things which we shouldn't consider funny,' he added shrewdly. 'This may be such an occasion.'

The forest gave way to a tapioca swamp, which in turn ended in a field of rice, nearly full grown but still green. Beyond it, at a distance of about a hundred yards, appeared a number of palm-thatched roofs. One was considerably larger than the rest.

'The major's bungalow,' said Li Chi, pointing, as the party halted at the edge of the rice.

'Is the river between us and the bungalow, or does it flow on the far side?' asked Biggles.

'The far side,' replied Li Chi.

Ayert spoke to him, and he translated: 'The *Lotus* is moored to a landing stage which is just above the bungalow.'

'Let's get nearer,' suggested Biggles—and then moved like lightning as from the branches of a tree that hung low overhead there came a sharp rustle. A second later, with a swish of twigs, a body dropped lightly to the ground.

For a moment the whole party looked startled. Then Li Chi spoke and the intrusion was at once explained. 'Lalla!' he exclaimed.

'Who are these people?' asked the new arrival breathlessly, in English, spoken with a peculiar accent.

'They are friends—British,' answered Li Chi. To the others he announced, 'This is Prince Lalla, Major Marling's son.'

Ginger gazed with curiosity on a young fellow of about his own age, slim, straight as a lance, dark-eyed, with skin as smooth as that of a girl. His dress was part European, part Eastern. A khaki shirt was thrust into well-worn riding breeches of the same colour, clipped tight into the waist by a belt which carried a heavy hunting knife with a jewelled handle. Mosquito boots encased his legs. On his head he wore a turban of blue silk, fastened across the front with a gold pin on which was mounted a ruby of considerable size. In the crook of his arm he held a light sporting rifle. He smiled half shyly, half sadly, at the visitors.

No time was wasted on conventional introductions. Nor did Biggles pay any heed to the rank, real or complimentary, of their reinforcement. 'What is happening at the bungalow?' he asked tersely.

'The Japanese have arrested my father,' answered Lalla. 'They have tied him to a tree, with the object, I think, of questioning him. He will not answer, so if they follow their usual methods they will torture him to make him speak. I was watching from the branches of this tree when I saw you emerge from the forest.'

'Where are your servants—the men of the village?'

questioned Biggles. 'Couldn't they have put up some sort of resistance?'

'Most of them were far away, working in the plantations,' explained Lalla. 'The house servants did what they could. From this tree you may see them lying dead in the compound. I myself was some distance away, riding my horse, when I heard shots. I galloped home to find out what was happening, but by that time the house had been seized.' Lalla drew from his shirt a small silver whistle. 'I could recall the labourers with this,' he went on, 'but the Japanese would also hear it, and understanding the meaning of it they would take steps to prevent us from organizing.'

'What are the Japs doing now—I mean, how are they disposed?' asked Biggles.

'Four remain on the launch to guard it. The others are doing what the beasts always do—eating and drinking, looting and destroying.'

'Have they posted sentries?'

'I did not observe any. Why should they trouble to post sentries here? What have soldiers to fear from a handful of native workmen armed only with swords and spears?'

Biggles smiled faintly. 'There are five of us now. We should be able to handle a simple operation like this. But I want one thing to be clearly understood. If we attack the Japanese here none must be allowed to escape to report our presence in the country. If that happened we should find it difficult, perhaps impossible, to get out. The failure of the Japanese to return must be attributed to hostile locals.'

Said Lalla grimly: 'If we can seize the launch I promise you that not one of them will reach the coast.

69

My foresters will hunt them down one by one and cut them to pieces.'

'That suits me,' returned Biggles. 'As a matter of fact, we could do with that launch ourselves. I have ideas about it. But let's get mobile, before the devils cut your father to pieces.'

'Why did you come here?' asked Lalla curiously.

Li Chi answered. 'They came to see your father about the scheme which we discussed some time ago.'

Lalla nodded. 'Ah! I understand.'

Biggles beckoned, and dropping on all fours began to make his way through the standing rice towards the bungalow. The others followed. Nothing more was said. In five minutes they were all at the far side of the field, lying flat in the lush growth, with Shansie village in plain view. Facing them at fifty paces, across a square compound of sun-baked earth, level and open except for an occasional tree, was the bungalow. The sides of the square were occupied by palm-thatched houses of simple design but good workmanship. With the exception of Major Marling, who had been lashed to a tree close by his own front door, the only living people in sight were Japanese soldiers. A number of dead men, presumably servants, lay where they had fallen. The enemy troops were standing about without any sort of order, some of them drinking, some eating food which they held in their hands, watching sinister preparations which, under the direction of an officer, were being made near the prisoner. A small fire had been lighted. Into it the point of a spear had been thrust. Laughing, the officer spoke. Biggles heard this, but not understanding the language he looked at Li Chi and raised his eyebrows.

'They know about the ruby mine,' translated Li Chi. 'That, no doubt, is why they are here. Major Marling has refused to tell them where it is located. They will torture him until he does.'

'Where precisely is the launch?' Biggles asked Lalla.

Lalla pointed. 'There, beyond the bungalow. You can't see it because the river flows through low ground.'

Biggles spoke to Ginger. 'Take Ayert with you and work your way round the back of the buildings to the launch. You ought to be able to take the guard by surprise. Scupper them, grab the launch, and stay on it. Your job then will be prevent anyone from getting aboard. The general idea is to get the enemy between two fires. We ought to drop half this bunch at the first rush. Get going. If possible I'll wait till I hear you shooting before I open up, but if they start on Marling I shall have to cut in. Get cracking.'

Li Chi explained the manœuvre to Ayert, who grinned, showing his yellow teeth, and followed Ginger, who was now crawling away, taking care to keep well within the rice.

Biggles lay still, watching the scene in front of him with cold hostile eyes. He had heard a lot about Japanese methods of waging war. Now he was confronted with an example, and its effect on him was to induce a feeling of ruthlessness. His fear at the moment was that the Japanese would begin work on their helpless captive before Ginger was in a position to attack the launch. And this, in fact, did happen. Five or six minutes after Ginger had left, the enemy officer drew the spear from the fire and examined the glowing point critically. It was clear from his manner that the next operation was going to provide him with considerable pleasure.

'So this is how the swine interrogate their prisoners?' muttered Biggles through his teeth. 'My God! It makes me go cold when I think that some of our fellows may have been treated like this. Well, although he doesn't know it, that little rat has finished his career as question master. For the first time in a long while shooting a man is going to give me the greatest satisfaction. This show has gone on long enough. Pick your man, and when I sound the gong, let drive.' He raised his rifle, snuggling the butt into his shoulder.

The officer approached his victim while the men, still eating and drinking, gathered round to form an appreciative audience.

Biggles' rifle cracked.

The Japanese officer jumped as though propelled by springs under his feet, throwing the spear high into the air. Landing, he spun round, staggered a little way and sprawled in the dust. Two of the spectators fell as the rifles of Li Chi and Lalla spoke. Biggles went on firing, quickly but deliberately, to take advantage of a situation that he knew could not last long. So far it was evident that the enemy had no idea of where the shots were coming from, and after the first shock of surprise had passed none of them tarried to find out. There was a general rush for cover, in the nature of a stampede; but before this was achieved three more were down. Another, limping, cried aloud in pain and fear as he stumbled on after his companions, who did nothing to help him. The survivors disappeared into, or in the region of the bungalow.

At this juncture shots from behind the building

72

announced that Ginger and Ayert were in action, although what was happening at the launch could not of course be seen.

Biggles sprang to his feet. 'Come on,' he called, 'let's finish the job.'

Lalla raised his whistle to his lips and blew a succession of short blasts.

'What's the idea?' demanded Biggles.

'That should bring our men into the fight,' was the answer. 'They won't be far away.'

This proved to be correct. A big man, sarong clad, dark-skinned, swinging a *parang*, dashed out of the forest yelling like a dervish.

'That's Malong, my foreman,' said Lalla, and called to him. More men appeared from various points.

Biggles did not wait to see what happened. He was anxious about Ginger and the launch. Followed by Li Chi he ran on, dashing across the open spaces between the huts, all the time working towards the rear of the big bungalow. One or two shots were fired, but they were wild and did no damage.

'They've lost their heads,' said Biggles.

'They'll lose their heads, literally, when Ayert and Malong get amongst them with their *parangs*,' prophesied Li Chi without emotion. 'The Japanese have lost their leader; the Shansians have found one. That will make a lot of difference.'

As it turned out, Ginger and Ayert were not in any need of help. When Biggles and Li Chi came into sight of the launch they were crouching behind the low bulwark. Seeing them, they stood up. Two Japanese lay dead on the river bank—the head of one some distance from the body.

'I see Ayert has been busy with his razor blade,' remarked Biggles in passing. To Ginger he called, 'Where's the rest of the guard?'

'The other two dived overboard and made for the bungalow. I wounded one of them,' answered Ginger.

'Lalla and his men will take care of them,' said Li Chi. 'It will probably be a gory business so I suggest we leave them to it.'

As if to confirm this statement shouts and cries came from the vicinity of the bungalow. Ayert, *parang* in hand, raced away in that direction.

'Yes, it sounds as if Lalla's boys are mopping up,' said Biggles. 'As far as the Japanese are concerned, I shan't saturate my handkerchief with tears on their account. They asked for what they're getting. Let's go and see how the big chief has fared.'

By the time they reached the compound the only sounds were those of pursuit. They found Major Marling rubbing chafed wrists as he spoke to his son, who stood beside him and had apparently just cut him free. He seemed no worse for his unpleasant adventure, and very little perturbed. But his expression, as his eyes surveyed the compound, where with cries of lamentation the bodies of the slain servants were being carried away by women, was grim.

'Barbarians,' he muttered savagely. 'These Japanese call themselves soldiers. Barbarians, that's what they are.' He turned to Li Chi. 'Did you see the way they used my people before they killed them?'

'No,' answered Li Chi softly.

'Prodded them with their bayonets. By God! I'll make them pay for this.' With a visible effort Major Marling resumed his composure. He turned to Biggles.

74

'I don't know who you are, sir, but I thank you for your timely intervention,' he said stiffly. 'Things were just beginning to look decidedly nasty when you opened fire. Well, the devils are now getting what they deserve. Did you see the way they were swilling my brandy? Scandalous behaviour! But come in, come in, and I'll see what I can do in the way of hospitality. Lalla, try to get hold of any servants who are left. Malong will take care of the pursuit. I expect the brutes have turned my house into a pigsty. No matter—we'll soon have it cleared up. I must apologise for this reception, gentlemen.'

'Don't mention it,' returned Biggles drily, winking at Ginger who was regarding their host with curiosity and not a little surprise, for he did not fill the picture he had imagined.

What he imagined does not matter. Major Marling was, in fact, a man of between fifty and sixty years of age, of medium height, slim—one might say dapper. He was still a good looking man in spite of the fact that his hair was snow white. His voice was crisp, brittle; he was obviously accustomed to being obeyed without question. He was dressed in a European flannel suit of semi-military cut, with white buckskin tennis shoes on his feet.

Apparently he became conscious of Ginger's scrutiny. 'What are you staring at, my boy? Don't you know it's rude to stare?' he asked sharply—so sharply that Ginger flushed.

'Yes, sir,' blurted Ginger.

'I should think so, by God!' snapped the major. 'But what are we standing here for? Let's get inside.' He led the way into the house.

# Chapter 8
# Decisions

Major Marling was right about the bungalow being a pigsty. Signs of the brief Japanese occupation were everywhere apparent. Not only had cupboards, chests and other receptacles, been ransacked in a frenzied search for loot, but much of the furniture had been wantonly smashed. However, some servants of both sexes appeared, and under the direction of one of their number proceeded to tidy up. Major Marling clapped his hands and gave an order, as a result of which, after a short delay, refreshments were brought.

'It appeared that they were about to do you a personal injury when we arrived, sir,' said Biggles.

'That was undoubtedly the intention,' asserted the Major. 'The rascals had heard about my rubies. I have some very fine ones, you know. Apart from these there is some very valuable jewellery that belonged to my wife. That confounded officer wanted to know where I kept the valuables. I wouldn't tell him—not me. No sir.'

'If they had learned about the rubies that would be sufficient reason for the raid,' opined Biggles. 'The question is, how did they learn about them?'

'No idea—no idea at all,' answered the major. 'My people are absolutely trustworthy. If it comes to that, they seldom go down the river.'

Biggles accepted a drink and looked at Li Chi. 'You may have been indirectly responsible,' he remarked.

Li Chi raised his eyebrows.

'You know about the rubies,' Biggles pointed out. 'So, presumably, did Ayert, since he came here with you. Did you ever speak of them when you returned to Elephant Island?'

'We may have done.'

'Then Pamboo may have overheard you talking. I'm beginning to wonder how much that fellow does know. One spy in a camp can learn a lot if he has the run of the place.'

Li Chi admitted the truth of this.

'What brought you fellows here, anyway?' demanded Major Marling. 'I don't encourage visitors, you know. I see by your uniforms that you're in the Air Force. Had a forced landing, perhaps?'

'No. We made a special trip to see you,' said Biggles.

Li Chi explained the object of the visit. 'Of course, this raid has altered the entire situation,' he concluded.

'Why has it?' asked the major curtly.

'I imagine you won't stay on here now, after what has happened today,' observed Biggles.

Major Marling flared up. 'And why not, sir? What the deuce do you take me for? Do I look the sort of man who would bolt at the first spot of bother—eh?'

'No,' conceded Biggles. 'But in view of what has just happened it may be supposed that you will have more unwelcome visitors at Shansie. I imagined—'

'Imagined what, sir?' broke in the major indignantly. 'My place is with my people so here I stay. There's nothing more to be said about it.'

Biggles shrugged. 'That's up to you, sir. I've nothing more to say. Sorry I raised the subject.'

'There's another reason why I should stay,' declared the major. 'You want more rubber don't you?'

'Yes—if you can get it.'

'Of course I can get it.'

'That's fine,' returned Biggles. 'But I can't see that it is going to be easy. You'll have more Japanese here. They're bound to send another party to find out what has become of this lot.'

'I shall be ready for them. They won't catch me napping twice. No sir.'

'Then the only problem that remains to be solved is this. How are we going to maintain contact with you? I'm thinking particularly of the rubber. I question whether your people will be able to get down to the coast and it's unlikely that we shall be able to get up the river a second time.'

'The enemy may not find it easy to discover what has happened to their first raiding party,' argued the major. 'All traces of the visit will be removed.'

'But the fact that you are British will be enough to warrant your arrest.'

'I may find it expedient to take steps to conceal my nationality—and I should have no difficulty in doing that.'

'How are you going to dispose of the launch?'

Major Marling rubbed his chin. 'Yes, that's a bit of a poser,' he admitted. 'No use trying to sink it. The river here isn't deep enough to cover it.'

'In that case we had better take it with us when we go,' announced Biggles. 'As a matter of fact I could probably find a use for it. Anyway, by using it we should make much faster time home than if we used the *kabang*. I understand the launch has a burden of fifty tons. We could take that much rubber with us if you feel inclined to let us have it?'

It was Li Chi's turn to look at Biggles askance. 'Are you thinking seriously of trying to take that vessel through the enemy forces stationed at the estuary? Tamashoa's headquarters is at Victoria Point, at the mouth of the river.'

'If we start fairly soon we should be at the estuary just before dawn, the darkest part of the night,' answered Biggles evenly. 'The usual river mist at that hour should also help to provide us with cover.'

'The Japanese will hear the engine even if they don't see the launch.'

'What of it? They'll be expecting the launch back, won't they?' Biggles smiled. 'The last thing to occur to them will be that it has changed hands.'

'Suppose we are challenged?'

'You mean—from the shore?'

'Yes.'

'You speak Japanese.'

'Yes.'

'Very well, you can answer.'

'And say what?'

'Anything you like. Say that we have orders to move to a new berth. By the time enquiries have been made we should be well out in the strait.'

Li Chi smiled. 'I once fooled a British gunboat like that. It might be done.'

'Then let's try it.'

'It's an audacious trick,' put in Major Marling.

'In my experience the more audacious the scheme

79

the more likely it is to succeed,' returned Biggles. 'It's the little things that go wrong—things within the limit of the enemy's imagination. What does exercise my mind is not getting out, but how we are to get back should occasion arise. We ought to have a line of communication with Shansie. A landing ground for aircraft would be the ideal thing, but I'm afraid the river here is too narrow, and winds about too much for a flying boat to get down on it.'

'I haven't a landing ground at the moment because the last thing I wanted here was any of those noisy devils' contraptions that you call aeroplanes,' said Major Marling. 'But no doubt something could be done.'

'What have you in mind?' asked Biggles curiously.

'By digging a trench I could drain the paddy fields to provide a hard level surface, if that is what you want. It would mean cutting the rice, but that doesn't matter. Alternatively I could break through the river bank just above here and flood the fields to a depth of two or three feet. Years ago we used to have serious floods, but by building an embankment we have been able to keep the river in its bed. A charge of dynamite would soon alter that.'

Biggles looked pleased. 'That's excellent, sir. It's all we should need. The machine I'm using at the moment for communication work is an amphibian, so I don't care whether the airfield is land or water.'

'Dry land would suit me better as a flood would make things more difficult for my people.'

'Very well, sir, I'll leave it to you,' decided Biggles. 'I take it that if I turn up here in an aircraft I shall find some sort of landing field available?'

'I'll see to it,' promised the major. 'There's just one other matter—a detail.' Addressing Li Chi he went on, 'I have here several Chinese and Lascars, the crew of a ship sunk by the enemy in the Gulf of Siam,* on the other side of the Isthmus. Reaching the shore they fled inland and eventually reached Shansie in a famished condition. They are not very happy here. I think they would prefer to do something more active, apart from which they are rather a drain on our resources. If you are going to take the launch it would seem to provide an opportunity for them to get out.'

'I could find work for them,' promised Li Chi. 'How many are there?'

'Sixteen—mostly greasers and stokers**—engine room crew, so I understand.'

'All right. With the approval of Squadron Leader Bigglesworth, if these men will put themselves under my orders, they may come.'

'Good. I shall be glad to get rid of them. They're an ugly looking crowd.'

'And now I have a request to make,' went on Li Chi. 'My fellows on Elephant Island are short of rifles. What about those we have captured today from the Japanese? Do you want them or may I have them?'

'Take them by all means,' offered the major. 'I certainly don't want them here. I don't want anything left about that might tell Japanese visitors what became of the men who arrived today.'

At this juncture Ayert returned, with Malong the

---

* Now the Gulf of Thailand
** Greasers kept the moving parts of the Engine room machinery well oiled, while the stokers kept the boilers full of coal.

overseer. They looked well satisfied with themselves. The survivors of the enemy force, they asserted, had been disposed of—although they did not put it like that. Their description of the final scene was lurid—a trifle too lurid, Ginger thought. Ayert was informed of the arrangements, and approved them.

'When do you intend to start?' the major asked Biggles.

'The sooner the better.'

'You'll stay for lunch, of course? It will take some little time to load up the rubber?'

'Thanks,' accepted Biggles.

'Then let us get the work in hand,' said Major Marling briskly.

Two hours later the *Lotus* cast off with the *kabang* in tow and headed downstream carrying fifty tons of fine crepe rubber, and the sixteen survivors of the ship that had been sunk in the Gulf of Siam. They were, Biggles remarked to Ginger, as tough-looking a pack of pirates as he had ever seen in one place. 'No wonder the major wanted to get rid of them,' he concluded, smiling.

Li Chi, who overheard this remark, surprised Ginger by observing, casually, that in his opinion they *were* pirates. He smiled at Ginger's expression and added: 'Oh yes, there are still plenty of pirates in the China Seas.'

'Better keep them away from those Japanese rifles,' said Biggles seriously.

'Don't worry about that,' returned Li Chi easily. 'These fellows will do as I tell them. If there is any trouble I'll let Ayert loose among them with his *parang*.' He walked over to the wheel which was being handled in a businesslike way by his ferocious-looking bosun.

Biggles smiled faintly as he lit a cigarette. 'We seem to have landed among some nice people,' he remarked to Ginger.

'The fellow I'm sorry for is Prince Lalla,' replied Ginger. 'I had a long talk with him after lunch. Nice lad. He's burning to get into the war. It's a pretty lonely sort of life for a chap of his age, stuck up here at the back of beyond.'

Biggles nodded, watching the monotonous river banks slide by. 'So I imagine,' he murmured.

Suddenly Ginger laughed quietly.

'What's funny?' inquired Biggles.

'Us,' answered Ginger. 'The things we do. To most people at home this part of the globe is now a place as inaccessible as the moon, crawling with Japanese; yet here we are, right in the middle of it, cruising along as if the country and the launch belonged to us.'

'As a matter of fact they do,' returned Biggles drily. 'The Japanese only borrowed them for a little while— a loan for which they'll have to pay a heavy rate of interest.'

After that they fell silent. The afternoon passed. The river rolled on, unchanging. The jungle steamed. The sun sank. Twilight dimmed the scene. The refugee crew disposed themselves in the bows, looking like heaps of dirty linen. Fireflies danced along the fringe of trees. The *Lotus* thrust its blunt nose into the stream, parting the turgid water. Biggles stood by the rail, smoking, deep in thought. Ginger lay down on the hard deck and fell asleep.

# Chapter 9
# Ayert Goes Ashore

Ginger awoke—or rather, was awakened—by a low murmur of voices. He got to his feet to find Biggles, Li Chi and Ayert, in earnest conversation. The murmur of their voices was the only sound. The engine had stopped. The *Lotus* drifted with barely perceptible movement on a sluggish tide, through grey wraiths of river mist.

'What's happened?' asked Ginger, suspecting a new development.

'We don't quite know,' replied Biggles. 'A little while ago a radio somewhere on board started buzzing out Morse. Li Chi found the instrument in a cabinet in the cabin. We should have guessed that there would be one on board. Li Chi picked up a signal from Victoria Point recalling the *Lotus* to base.'

'What have you done about it?'

'Li Chi acknowledged the signal—it was all he could do.'

'Then there's no harm done?'

'We're not sure about that. Listening, Li Chi has picked up other signals. As they stand they are vague, but it seems that some sort of operation is in progress near Japanese headquarters at Victoria Point. We shall have to pass near the place on the way out.'

'Then we may see something.'

'The enemy may see us, too, and that's something

we want to avoid. We were just discussing the advisability of sending Ayert ashore to find out just what is going on. We are not far from the estuary. Ayert says he can get the information from the Chinese labourers' quarters. Moreover, he might learn the location of enemy posts on the river banks. It would be useful to know that because it would enable us to set a course to keep clear of them.'

Ginger looked at his watch and saw that it was just three o'clock. 'What does Li Chi think?'

'He's in favour of Ayert going ashore.'

'We've nothing to lose by the delay, provided Ayert doesn't take too long over his reconnaissance,' observed Ginger.

'We must be across the strait before dawn.' Biggles spoke briefly to Li Chi , with the result that the engine was started, and as the *Lotus* moved her nose was turned towards the northern bank. Ayert dropped overboard, waded ashore and disappeared in the mist.

The others waited, listening; but no sound came. To Ginger it was a tedious vigil. He was tired; the river mist was dank and chill and the mosquitoes were vicious. Ayert was away about an hour. He returned silently, as he had departed. Ignoring the others he spoke swiftly and at some length to Li Chi. It was evident from his manner that the information he had to convey was urgent and important, and Ginger fidgeted with impatience as he waited to learn what it was. Li Chi, his hands thrust in voluminous sleeves, translated.

'I am to blame,' he began, with acid hostility. 'I should have taken the head from the shoulders of that misbegotten cur.'

'Who are you talking about?' asked Biggles, somewhat taken aback by this unusual tone of voice.

'Pamboo. He is swaggering about with the enemy, having told them all he knows. Ayert got the news from some coolies who were on night work.'

'How much has Pamboo told them—that's the point?' inquired Biggles.

'As you thought, he was responsible for the raid on Shansie. He has told them that I am hiding on Elephant Island, where British officers have now arrived in an aeroplane.'

'I suppose there's no doubt about this?'

'None whatsoever. Victoria Point is buzzing with the news. The labourers of course, are hoping that the British are about to deliver an attack to drive out the Japanese. This is not all. It is known that the sawmill is working and that I am building a new junk to take away a large store of rubber which I have collected.'

'In short,' murmured Biggles, 'the skunk has spilled the entire can of beans?'

'I should have removed the intestines from the despicable creature,' grated Li Chi.

'You may still have an opportunity,' remarked Biggles dispassionately.

'I doubt it,' was the reply. 'Our entire scheme is torn wide open.'

'Fiddlesticks,' snapped Biggles.

'But wait until you've heard the rest,' returned Li Chi curtly. 'The upshot of all this is, a Japanese landing is about to be made on Elephant island. The force is being assembled at Victoria Point. A ship has been brought from Penang to take the troops over. It is already here.'

'A ship, eh? What sort of ship?'

'The *Sumatran*, a coastal supply vessel of a thousand tons. She carries guns fore and aft and has anti-aircraft deck armament. My friend, I'm afraid your long journey has been in vain.'

'When I'm ready to throw in the sponge I'll let you know,' asserted Biggles evenly. 'When is this assault timed to take place—today?'

'No, tomorrow night.'

'Not until tomorrow! Why, that gives us plenty of time to do something about it. Where is this ship?'

'Lying in the channel about a mile off shore. I expect she'll come in late tonight at high water to pick up the troops.'

'What time is high water?'

'Ten o'clock.'

Biggles thought for a little while. 'That gives us nearly twenty hours. I think this ship, the *Sumatran* would be very useful to us,' he observed.

Li Chi was for once startled from his habitual calm. 'You have a touch of fever, I think.'

'On the contrary, I've never felt better in my life,' declared Biggles lightly. 'Tell me; you know these waters. What sort of crew would the *Sumatran* carry?'

'A Japanese crew, now, with Japanese officers, I expect.'

'How many?'

'Twenty, perhaps.' Li Chi regarded Biggles with suspicion not unmixed with apprehension. 'If you tell me that you are going to try to sink the *Sumatran* I shall know that you are ill in the intestines.'

'Sink her! Good Lord, no! Not on your life. Incidentally, I have every reason to suppose that my intestines are in very good order. But it seems to me that we might employ the *Sumatran* to good purpose. There's nothing like improving your position as occasion offers. We started with a *kabang*. We moved up a step when we took the launch. Obviously the next step is up the side of the *Sumatran*.'

'And so on to the *Queen Mary*?' Li Chi was getting sarcastic.

'If it suited my purpose—yes.'

'And what is your purpose?'

Biggles frowned. 'Come, come, Li Chi. You haven't forgotten that I was sent here to get rubber? I've no intention of going back without any.'

'At the rate you're going it seems likely that you won't go back at all.'

'There is always that risk, I admit,' said Biggles. 'That's what I'm paid for.'

Li Chi shrugged. 'Proceed,' he invited helplessly. 'I have taken risks in my time, but I perceive that our brains work in different grooves. What is your purpose with the *Sumatran*?'

'There are several purposes staring us in the face. First, if we take the ship we shall deny the enemy the use of it. Secondly, such a vessel might save my fellows an awful lot of work—as you may see in due course. And thirdly—and this is perhaps the most important— we shall hold up the proposed Japanese invasion of Elephant Island.'

'You still intend going on with the scheme, then?'

'I see no reason yet for abandoning it. It's a pity that the Japs had to find out about us, but that was bound to happen sooner or later. The fact that it has happened sooner than we expected has merely put the clock forward. The automatic answer to that is, we must work faster. I'm thinking on those lines now. Things might be a lot worse. We do at least know what the enemy is doing. He might have taken us by surprise. As it is, by knowing his moves we should be able to forestall them.'

'But this is making it all very difficult.'

'From what I've seen of it, in war nothing is easy.' said Biggles.

'Are you going to attack the *Sumatran* now?'

'No. I'm not quite ready. We've plenty of time and there are things to be done at Elephant Island. Let's get going or we shall have daylight on us. Getting back to the island is the first job. If we are challenged I shall leave it to you to do the talking.'

Li Chi touched Ayert on the arm and together they walked to the wheel. The engine came to life, and in another minute the launch was gliding through the mist towards the estuary. Ginger stood by the rail, staring towards the unseen shore. Biggles remained with him. For some time neither spoke.

'What do you really intend doing with the *Sumatran*?' asked Ginger softly, at last. 'Grabbing her seems a pretty desperate scheme to me.'

'I don't agree,' returned Biggles. 'I reckon the ship is a gift from the gods and I'm going to accept it. The thing should be simple. Consider it. The Japanese won't be expecting trouble. Here, in home waters, they'll hardly bother to keep watch, if I know anything about them. There should be plenty of tough fighters amongst Li Chi's old crew on the island. Then, look at this bunch of cut-throat pirates we've got on board. Wait till I tell them that if they can get the *Sumatran* to

India there will be a nice packet of prize money to share out—then watch their faces.'

'Did you say *India*?'

'You heard me. This ship's a thousand tonner. We'll stuff her so full of rubber that she'll bounce over the waves. If she can shift a thousand tons, that will be so much less for us to cart across the drink in the Liberators.'

'Phew! I didn't think of that,' muttered Ginger. 'But she'll be spotted by enemy machines. They're bound to look for her.'

'Exactly. That's the snag—and, incidentally, why I didn't attack right away,' said Biggles. 'We might hide the *Lotus* at Elephant Island, but we couldn't do that with the *Sumatran*, so for the moment she is better where she is. If we grab her soon after dark tonight we shall have the whole night in front of us to get her loaded and away on a course for India.'

'But when it gets light she'll still be within range of enemy aircraft, and they'll be looking for her,' Ginger pointed out.

'Fine. You're keeping pace with the argument. But by that time I hope to have a brace of Lightnings on the spot to take care of any interference.'

'How are you going to get them here?'

'Algy and Bertie should be back by now. Someone will have to take the Gosling to India to fetch the Lightnings out.'

'That will be all right if the runway is far enough advanced for them to land on it.'

'It should be, from what Li Chi said about it. That's another reason why I decided to leave the *Sumatran* where she is for the time being. I want to see how far they've got with the runway.'

'Lightnings won't be able to escort the *Sumatran* all the way to India.'

'It shouldn't be necessary. Whoever goes across in the Gosling can pass word to the navy. They'll send machines of the Fleet Air Arm out to watch her, and, I hope, a couple of destroyers to take her in.'

'Can we get mixed up with the navy?'

'I don't care who we get mixed up with as long as we get the rubber across,' declared Biggles. 'I think the navy will see it in that light, too. Hello,—here we go.'

A voice had hailed from somewhere in the darkness on the starboard side. Li Chi answered and a short conversation ensued. What was said neither Biggles nor Ginger knew, the talk being carried on presumably in Japanese. When it ended Li Chi joined them.

'What was all that about?' asked Biggles.

'Someone advised us to heave to until morning on account of the mist,' answered Li Chi.

'They identified us by the engine, I suppose?'

'They couldn't do otherwise; the *Lotus* is the only craft up the river.'

Nothing more was said. Ginger stared into the gloom, wondering how Ayert found his way, for all that could be seen was an occasional vague glimpse of palm fronds against the sky. Odd sounds came from the river bank. Sometimes voices could be heard, but the *Lotus* was not challenged. She chugged on.

A slight to and fro rocking motion and a thinning of the mist told Ginger that they were leaving the estuary for the open sea; and he was just about to make a remark to this effect to Biggles when a huge grey shape loomed ahead. There was a sudden shout. Ayert flung the wheel hard over, and the *Lotus* veered past a big ship lying at anchor with a narrow margin to spare. A stream of vituperation followed the launch as it held on its course.

'That must have been the *Sumatran*,' said Li Chi.

Biggles smiled. 'We nearly boarded her before we were ready.'

'Ayert did not know her exact position,' explained Li Chi.

'He knows it now,' murmured Biggles.

The *Lotus* chugged on, rocking now as she rode a slight swell in the strait. The mist cleared. Stars appeared overhead with the Southern Cross gleaming. The dark bulk of the forest-clad hills of Elephant Island rose from the western horizon.

'Where are we making for?' Biggles asked Li Chi.

'There's a sheltered cove on the far side that should suit us well,' was the answer. 'The water runs deep so we can take her in close to the shore. It is where I am building the junk.'

'I leave it to you,' said Biggles. 'You'd better make a signal when we get near or someone may take a shot at us, thinking we are a Japanese patrol.'

'I had thought of it,' replied Li Chi.

Biggles yawned. 'I think we've done a useful trip,' he remarked. 'Gosh! I'm sleepy.'

'Sez you,' muttered Ginger. 'I must keep awake long enough though to see Bertie's face when we arrive home in this cruiser.'

# Chapter 10
# Preparations

Having gone ashore Biggles and Ginger were walking towards Li Chi's house when they met Algy and Bertie coming to meet them, for it turned out that they had been told of the party's return in a Japanese launch. Dawn was just breaking. Li Chi had remained behind to supervise the unloading of the rubber and the camouflaging of the *Lotus*.

'I say, old boy, where did you pick up the yacht?' asked Bertie enthusiastically.

'We asked the Japs to lend it to us—and we asked in a way that made it difficult for them to say no,' answered Biggles cheerfully. 'When did you get back?'

'Late last night,' answered Algy. 'There have been several enemy machines—mostly Zeros*—over, having a look round.'

'We must expect that,' returned Biggles. 'Things are happening.'

'Did you see Marling?'

'Yes.' On the way to the house Biggles narrated briefly the events at Shansie. Having gone into the lounge and made themselves comfortable, he resumed.

---

* Common name for Japanese single-seat Mitsubishi 'Zeke' type O fighter armed with two machine guns synchronised to fire through the propellers and two 20mm Cannon in the wings. See cover illustration.

'There are several things I'm anxious to know. First, how goes the runway?'

'It's advanced enough for single landings, as long as the pilot knows where to look for it. I wouldn't say it's ready for the Liberators, but fighters could get in. It ought to be ready for the Liberators by tonight. Work on it never stops.'

'Good! Did you bring any petrol back with you?'

'As much as we could stow away in four-gallon cans.'

'What's the position in India?'

'The gang is all ready, waiting for the word to bring the machines over.'

'We're doing fine,' declared Biggles. 'And we shall have to continue like that if we are to get this thing buttoned up. Now listen, everybody. It's becoming increasingly clear that due to the activities of this skunk Pamboo we shan't be able to hang around here for as long as we expected; but we'll carry on as long as we can. The only thing that matters is the rubber and we've got to be prepared to take chances in order to get it to India; but I doubt if we shall be able to shift five thousand tons before this place is made too hot to hold us—certainly not if we are to rely entirely on air transportation. There may be other ways. For instance, there's a thousand ton enemy supply ship lying off Victoria Point. I aim to snaffle her tonight. To get a thousand tons of rubber off our hands at one go would give us a flying start.'

'By gad! I should jolly well think so—absolutely,' declared Bertie warmly, polishing his eyeglass vigorously. 'Do we come on this show?'

'Sorry, no. You'll have to go back to India to get a couple of Lightnings across. We shall need them.'

Bertie's face fell. 'Couldn't we call the boys by radio?'

'We could—and tell the Japs where we are and what we are doing,' said Biggles sarcastically. 'I'm not going to risk that.'

'Why do you want the Lightnings in such a hurry?' asked Algy.

'I'll tell you,' answered Biggles. 'This is my plan. As soon as it gets dark I'm going to grab the *Sumatran*—that's the ship—and bring her here. The work of loading her with the stuff they make tennis balls out of will begin right away. It might be possible to finish the job by dawn, but I doubt it. By that time the Japanese will be in a flap looking for her, and as we can't hide a ship that size it won't be long before they spot her. Now, if we've got the Lightnings here we ought to be able to knock down Japanese reconnaissance machines before they can get the information back to Tamashoa's head-quarters—get the idea? Moreover, the *Sumatran* will need air cover in case the Japanese spot her heading westward and decide to drop cookies* on her. Frankly, I don't think they'll do that, because for one thing they won't know what has happened, and for another, they'll hesitate to bomb what they imagine is their property. But the Lightnings will have to escort her until she's outside the range of enemy bombers. Now you see why it is vital that we should have the fighters here.'

'Who's going to take the *Sumatran* to India?' asked Algy.

'We shall have to fix that up with Li Chi. We're not capable of handling a big ship.'

* R.A.F. slang for bombs.

'Assuming Li Chi goes, how is he going to get back?'

'I was just coming to that. I'm hoping it won't be necessary for him to go all the way to India. The first thing you do when you get across is get in touch with the navy people; tell them what's happened and ask them to send a destroyer out to pick up the *Sumatran*. Ask the Air Officer Commanding India to notify Raymond so that he can fix things with the Admiralty. If the navy will take over the ship it ought to be possible to pick up Li Chi in the Gosling and bring him straight back. I think we might take a chance and tell the boys they can make a trial run with the Liberators tomorrow unless they hear from us that they are not to start. Get back youself as soon as you can. Taffy Hughes and Ferocity Ferris had better bring the Lightnings across. They should be here before you. We'll be on the watch for them and make a smudge fire to show them where they are to land. Actually, there are two reasons why we must grab the *Sumatran*. I've told you one. The other is because the Japanese are planning an invasion of Elephant Island and I'm hoping that the loss of the transport ship will set them back at least a week. Before that time is up we may be able to hit them another crack. I've spoken to Li Chi about his putting spies on the mainland to keep us notified of enemy movements. In a couple of days we ought to have the Liberators on the job shifting the rubber. That's all.'

'Will Tamashoa wait a week before he attacks?' queried Algy dubiously.

'I think so—if he knows his job. Admittedly, he knows—or he soon will know—that a British force is here but he won't know in what strength. He's bound to try to get that information before he attacks.'

Algy nodded and glanced through the window at the sky, now turquoise blue. 'Okay. We'd better get off right away.' He looked at his watch. 'It's just turned six. By flying flat out I ought to be across soon after twelve. The Lightnings should be here between four and five. I'm afraid it will be dark before I get back.'

'Why not wait until tomorrow?'

'I'd rather get back.'

'As you like. We'll put flares out for you. Bring some petrol with you. Shortage of fuel at this juncture is likely to be one of our problems.'

Algy turned. 'I could bring more out if I left Bertie here. That's really no need for him to come.'

'It's a longish trip. You'll get a bit browned off by yourself, won't you?'

'Naturally, I'd rather have company, but if it means a bigger load of petrol—well, I'll go solo.'

'Here, I say, old boy, that's a bit tough on you,' broke in Bertie. 'You stay here and have a rest. I'll go.'

'We'll soon settle that,' decided Biggles. He put his hand in his pocket and took out a coin. 'Heads—Algy goes; tails—Bertie.' He tossed the coin. 'Heads it is. Algy goes. Bertie, you'll stay. No doubt we can find you a job.'

Algy turned to the door. 'See you later,' he said, and went out.

'Watch your step until you're out of the danger area,' Biggles called after him. 'Enemy air activity may be getting lively.'

'I'll watch it.' With a wave Algy took the path to the lake.

'Does this mean I can come on the show tonight?' asked Bertie.

'If you like.'

'By jove! That's marvellous—absolutely marvellous. Poor old Algy. Dashed hard work, this roaring to and fro across all those miles of drink.'

'We knew that before we started,' asserted Biggles. 'I fancy we shall be sick of the sight of the Indian Ocean, or any other ocean, before we're through with this operation.'

Li Chi came in and reported that the launch had been hauled close inshore, and so covered with verdure that he was not sure if he himself would ever find it again.

'In that case you'd better start looking,' answered Biggles smiling. 'We shall need her tonight.'

'All hands are at work on the runway and listening posts have been established to report the approach of enemy aircraft,' said Li Chi.

'Good work,' commended Biggles. 'With luck we shall have the Liberators operating sometime to-morrow. As long as they can land and get off again that's all that matters—they will never be here longer than is absolutely necessary. By the way, Li Chi, assuming that we get the *Sumatran*, where do you suggest we put her? Which is the best place for loading?'

'The cove where we have moored the *Lotus*. It has this advantage. The rubber is not far away. My junk is in the same cove.'

'I see.' Biggles then explained his plan in detail and concluded by asking Li Chi if he or Ayert, the only master mariners available, would mind taking the

*Sumatran* to India, pointing out that naval co-operation might make it unnecessary for him to go all the way.

Li Chi expressed his willingness to do this.

'Then that's about all we can do for the time being,' said Biggles. 'The next thing is to get some sleep. I'll leave it to you to chosse the best men for the attack on the *Sumatran*.'

'How many shall we need?'

'Are you coming?'

Li Chi smiled. 'It will be like old times.'

'Fine. A score of men should be enough. The ideal thing would be to choose men who know how to work a ship. Those men we brought from Shansie should be useful. Marling said that some of them were engine room men. If we get away with the ship they could stay on board. There should be a nice parcel of prize money for them to share out, later on.'

Li Chi bowed. 'I'll see to it. One other thing. These Liberators that are coming. Will there be crews with them—gunners, and so on? I ask because if so it will be necessary to prepare accommodation.'

'No,' answered Biggles. 'What little servicing will have to be done here we can do ourselves. The machines carry enough fuel for the round trip. Overhauls or repairs will have to be done at the base in India.'

After this debate Biggles and Ginger went off to snatch a few hours sleep, leaving Bertie on duty, to rouse them should any development occur. When they awoke, late in the afternoon, he had nothing to report except that work had been suspended several times due to the proximity of enemy aircraft; some had been sighted; some had made a reconnaissance of the island. 'Looking for their bally lugger,' conjectured Bertie.

'They'll be looking for bigger fish by tomorrow, I hope,' remarked Biggles, putting on his shoes.

'The *Sumatran* is still in the same place.'

'How do you know?'

'You can see her through Li Chi's binoculars from the top of the hill. We've just had a dekko* at her.'

Li Chi came in to announce that all arrangements for the raid were complete. The men had been detailed and were looking forward to it. 'Seizing a ship is a thing they understand,' said he, ingenuously. 'We Chinese believe it is a good thing to start an enterprise with full stomachs,' he went on. 'Dinner will be served in a few minutes.'

'I'm ready,' Biggles assured him.

Half way through the meal there came an interruption. It was expected, and the roar of low-flying planes sent them running out to see two Lightnings circling round, wing tip to wing tip.

Those on the ground ran down to the lake, lit a smudge fire and took up positions on the edge of the runway to make its position clear. The fighters landed, and under Biggles' directions taxied to the frame shelter that had been prepared. Taffy Hughes and Ferocity Ferris, smiling broadly, jumped down, both talking at once, obviously in high spirits.

'See anything on your way over?' asked Biggles, when greetings had been exchanged.

'Water, look you—nothing whatever but water,' said Taffy in a disgusted voice.

* Slang: a look.

'Where did it all come from?' asked Ferocity, plaintively.

'No one knows. Perhaps there was nowhere else to put it,' returned Biggles brightly. 'Come up to the mess and have a plate of fish with bamboo shoots.'

'How about filling the machines' tanks first?' suggested Taffy.

'No hurry about that. They won't be needed until morning. Speaking of petrol, go easy on it; we've none to waste.'

'Algy's bringing some more across,' stated Ferocity.

'Had he started back when you left?'

'No, but he reckoned he wouldn't be long.'

'Did he tell you what was cooking?'

'You bet he did.'

'Then there is no need for me to repeat the story,' said Biggles.

'Are we going on this show tonight?' inquired Taffy.

'No,' replied Biggles. 'You'll stay here and have a nice night's sleep. You may have plenty to do in the morning?'

'Doing what?'

'Starting at the crack of dawn you'll take turns doing patrols at twenty thousand over the island to deal with any intruder who tries to get a squint at what's going on here. It shouldn't be difficult. The fellow in the aircraft won't be expecting you. He'll be looking down at us. You'll be looking down at him. The great thing always to remember is, we don't want our machines to be seen landing or taking off from here. The longer we can keep the enemy guessing the better. But time's going. We shall soon have to get cracking. Algy won't be here for some time yet. If he's late we shan't be able to wait for him. Where the *Sumatran* is concerned every hour of darkness counts. If we go before he comes you'll have to put marker flares out for him. You'll hear him coming.'

This Taffy and Ferocity promised to do.

Twilight was falling when the conference came to an end.

# Chapter 11

# Ginger Gets a Shock

At eight o'clock, in the heavy sultry darkness that marks the first hours of tropic light, by the light of a firebrand Biggles inspected his commandos and expressed himself satisfied. The inspection took place in a forest glade near the cove in which the *Lotus* had been hidden.

The scene was one Ginger would never forget. It was one that few white men are privileged to witness, and in modern times might occur once in a lifetime. The selected men, a round score of them, standing in a rough line leaning on their weapons, were as motley a crowd as a Hollywood film director could have imagined; as ill-dressed and ill-shod a gang as Morgan's buccaneers must have been after their march to sack Panama. The flickering yellow light of the torch fell on shining sweaty faces that were all shades between yellow and brown. For the most part they wore the *sarong*, or the ragged remains of one; but in addition, as if in honour of the occasion, each man had produced some piece of frippery with which to bedeck himself—a brilliant sash or a gaudy handkerchief. For weapons each warrior had made his own choice, and the result was, to say the least of it, spectacular. Cold steel, in the form of *parangs*, or the ghastly Malay *kriss**, was conspicuous, for in view of the proximity of the enemy coast Li Chi had pointed out the necessity for silent action. White teeth flashed in eager anticipation of the onset which—as Li Chi said—was the sort of warfare these men understood, the sort that had been played by their ancestors for centuries, even until recent times. If, said he naively, they had made piracy a national sport among themselves, how much greater must be their satisfaction in having this opportunity to strike back at the rabble that had overrun their country, burnt their kampongs** and seized their sampans***?

Ayert, making the air reek with one of his enormous home-made cigars, his mutilated face looking more demoniacal than ever, limped up and down the line keeping some sort of order—at no small risk, it seemed to Ginger, of losing his remaining eye; for from time to time a pirate would swish his *parang* through the air, either to test it as a musician might tune his instrument before a concert, or out of sheer light-heartedness. Li Chi, still in his yellow kimono, stood watching, calm, his face expressionless.

The background was appropriate to the scene. The towering trunks of forest trees, overhung and looped with the endless rattans, might have been the masts of a fleet of sailing ships, with rigging awry after an action. Lower, through the fronds of the decorative tree-ferns, fireflies flickered like will-o'-the-wisps.

The three officers who were to accompany the raid

* A very sharp Malay dagger with a wavy blade.
** Hamlet or village.
*** A name applied to any small boat of Chinese pattern.

would not have passed muster for a ceremonial parade. All were without jackets, shirt sleeves rolled, throats bare, waists belted to carry small-arms. Their faces, arms and necks had been blackened with charcoal, commando style, not for effect, but because white skin can be seen at night more easily than black. Taffy and Ferocity stood on one side, watching, as did the entire population of the island, comprising, as it was now revealed, more than a hundred men. They had paused in the labour of piling Li Chi's rubber at the water edge ready for loading into the *Sumatran*. Algy had not yet returned. Biggles decided not to wait for him. 'We ought to be back in a couple of hours or so,' he told Taffy.

'I hope so, by gad,' muttered Bertie. 'I feel an absolute scallywag. If my old mare could see me she'd jump clean over the paddock gate.'

'You asked to come,' Biggles pointed out.

'Oh yes, rather. Wouldn't miss this show for worlds—no bally fear,' returned Bertie. 'But I wish it wasn't so beastly hot.'

Biggles turned to Li Chi. 'The men know exactly what they are to do?'

'To the letter. My friend, not even you could teach them anything about this business.'

'And you have decided on your answer when we are challenged?'

'I shall say that we are having engine trouble and that I wish to come on board to speak to the chief engineer. There should be no difficulty about that. Boats have been passing between the shore and the ship so I feel sure the landing ladder will be down.'

'Then we needn't waste any more time,' said Biggles.

'Let's get off.' He turned towards the *Lotus*, now stripped of its covering of branches.

There was a general move in the same direction. As soon as the officers were on board the troops swarmed over the rail with an agility that was obviously the result of long practice.

'Beats me how the blighters don't cut themselves with their bally side-arms,' murmured Bertie, looking rather ridiculous with his monocle in his eye the better to watch the proceedings.

'Don't forget to keep an ear open for Algy,' was Biggles' last injunction to those ashore.

Ayert started the engine. The screw churned the water and the *Lotus* chugged busily towards open water. The canopy of forest trees fell away. Stars appeared. The moon had not yet risen. The bows of the little vessel swung round and she stood out to sea. But not for long; for as soon as she was clear, Ayert took up a course parallel with the coast, it being necessary to round the island in order to reach the strait. Li Chi spoke to the storming party who at once fell silent, disposing themselves, sitting or lying close under the rail, where they would not be seen by those on board the *Sumatran* as they approached the taller vessel.

The distance to the firefighter as a bird would fly was roughly nine miles, but taking into account the preliminary rounding of the island the distance was nearer twelve. Of these the first ten were covered in less than an hour, for the sea was flat calm and Ayert gave the engine all it would take; but he now slowed to half speed, and after a while, by manoeuvring the throttle, caused the engine to run irregularly, to create an impression of trouble. His good eye probed the darkness ahead. Presently he grunted and altered course a trifle. Looking in the new direction Ginger could just make out the bulk of the ship, about half a mile distant. Its outline hardened as they drew nearer. Noises came out of the night. An engine room bell rang musically; a chain rattled.

'Is that ship moving?' Biggles asked Li Chi anxiously.

'No, but she's getting ready to go,' was the answer. 'They're weighing anchor, no doubt to move in close to Victoria Point. We cut it fine, but we're in time.'

Possibly because of the activity on the *Sumatran*, resulting in careless watch-keeping, it was some time before the *Lotus* was seen. She was within a cable's length* before she was hailed.

Ayert held on his course, and there was a brief delay before another hail came through the night air. This time it was a definite challenge, or at any rate, a warning, for the *Lotus* was now so close that water dripping from the *Sumatran's* anchor could be plainly heard. Li Chi answered, and a conversation ensued between him and someone on the deck of the *Sumatra* — probably the officer of the watch. What the actual words were that passed Ginger never knew, but the general trend was fairly clear. Li Chi was explaining the arrival of the *Lotus* which, with its engine cut, still had enough way on it to reach the boarding gangway.

The moment the two vessels touched, Ayert let go the wheel, and with a bound made fast. He finished this with a sort of hiss, and this was the signal for a spectacle that left Ginger slightly breathless. He

* A nautical measurement, about 180 metres.

expected that they, the leaders of the expedition, would be first up the steps; and Biggles had in fact announced this to be his intention; but in the rush that now occurred they were nearly knocked down. There was no stopping it. Biggles dare not appeal to Li Chi for fear of being heard by those on the *Sumatran*.

Ayert went up the side of the ship like a cat going up a garden fence. Li Chi was close behind him. There was a shout, cut short; then a murmur of confusion rising to a considerable noise before starting to recede. Behind Li Chi poured the pirates. They flung themselves over the rail. Naturally, Biggles, Ginger and Bertie followed as quickly as they could—Biggles muttering his displeasure at the turn things had taken, the result, he asserted with asperity, of employing an undisciplined mob. By the time they reached the deck there was little to be seen. Three Japanese sailors lay prone. Sounds alone gave an indication of what was happening, and there were not so many of these as might have been expected. Most of them came from below—shouts, cries, snarls and an occasional thud. It struck Ginger that most of the crew must have been below, or had fled down the companion way when the pirates swarmed aboard, either to escape or to fetch weapons which in the ordinary way would not be carried. Anyhow, the pirates, who seemed to know how to find their way about a ship, had gone down to rout them out.

Pistol in hand, Biggles ran towards the superstructure in which the bridge was situated. The others, having nothing better to do, followed him. Having reached the bridge there was still nothing for them to do. Ayert and Li Chi were there. Ayert was calmly wiping his *parang* on his sarong. Two Japanese, an officer and a rating, lay on the floor in a widening pool of blood. Ginger shuddered.

'Foolishly they aimed their pistols at us,' murmured Li Chi, as if this was all the explanation needed.

'Hit 'em. Like Clark Gable, *tuans*,' said Ayert, grinning, showing his yellow teeth.

'I will go to see what happens below decks,' decided Li Chi.

Biggles nodded. 'From what I could hear your fellows won't need any help from us. I think we'll stay here. I have a feeling that things will be a bit messy downstairs.'

'War is always a messy business, my friend, no matter where it is; and the *parang* is no more barbarous than the bomb, the tank or the flame thrower, such as the *civilized* peoples of Europe use,' said Li Chi stiffly, with emphasis on the word civilized. He went off while Biggles, Bertie and Ginger returned to the deck. Presently the pirates came drifting back in ones and twos, laughing. Li Chi returned to report that the ship was theirs. Steam had already been raised to take the ship to the port of embarkation. The engine room crew were standing by—the pirate crew—waiting for the order to start.

Biggles turned his eyes to the shore in a penetrating stare. 'I wonder if they heard anything there,' he conjectured. 'I don't think there's any point in waiting to find out. Ginger, it would be a good idea if you went below and took over the radio. If you pick up any signals let me know, and I'll ask Li Chi to come down and translate.'

Ginger had no difficulty in finding the radio room. A telegraph was buzzing so he hurried back to the deck, with the result that Li Chi was soon at the instrument. For a little while he listened, face expressionless, making notes in Chinese characters on the scribbling pad.

Ginger smiled as he looked at the strange writing. 'What's all that about?' he inquired. 'Anything that concerns us?'

'It will concern you very much,' answered Li Chi quietly. 'The signal is from the leader of a Japanese destroyer flotilla.* The commander reports that he found a British aircraft of the Gosling type adrift on the water at a point about three hundred miles east of Mergui. There was one pilot in the aircraft. He was picked up and taken prisoner. The aircraft was sunk by gunfire.'

Ginger felt the blood drain from his face. The muscles seemed to go stiff. For a few seconds he could not speak. 'Was the name of the prisoner given?' he blurted.

'No.'

'It doesn't matter,' muttered Ginger. 'There could be only one Gosling in that area. They've got Algy. Was there anything else?'

'Yes,' returned Li Chi imperturbably. 'The ship asked for instructions about the disposal of the prisoner. The answer came from Singapore. The ship was ordered to take the prisoner to the nearest base for questioning. The flotilla is therefore proceeding to Victoria Point where it expects to arrive tomorrow afternoon.'

'Thanks,' said Ginger in a dull voice. He tore back

* A fleet of small ships.

to Biggles. 'The Japanese have got Algy,' he reported. 'A destroyer picked him up out of the drink and is taking him to Victoria Point.' He gave the details.

Biggles tapped a cigarette on the back of his hand and then threw it into the sea. He did not speak.

'What are we going to do about it?' asked Ginger desperately.

'I don't quite know—yet,' replied Biggles. 'Obviously, we can't take on a flotilla of destroyers in this tub. The first thing is to get her away with the rubber. When we've done that we'll see what can be done. You say the flotilla will arrive tomorrow afternoon?'

'So Li Chi said.'

'Nothing much can happen to Algy between now and then. We'll get back to the island,' decided Biggles.

Li Chi appeared.

'Anything else?' asked Biggles.

'Tamashoa has made a signal to the flotilla leader asking that great care be taken of the prisoner as he wishes to question him personally.'

'I see,' murmured Biggles. 'All right. Take the ship across to the island. Quite apart from Algy these destroyers are a new menace. Good thing we learned about them or the *Sumatran* might have sailed slap into them on her way to India. As it is, Tamashoa may send them in pursuit of the *Sumatran* as soon as he tumbled to what has happened.' He stared again towards the shore, a dark indistinct mass running down the eastern side of the strait. A signal lamp* was

---

* Before the radio communication was common on ships, signal lamps were often used to send messages between ships by flashing morse code signals. They are still in use today where radio is unsafe or unusable.

winking. 'That must be somebody talking to us,' he observed. 'What's he saying?'

'I was reading it,' returned Li Chi. 'Someone is asking why the ship does not come in.'

'Can we be seen from the shore do you think?'

'I doubt it, at this distance.'

'We shall have to answer the signal or they may get suspicious,' resolved Biggles. 'I noticed a lamp on the bridge. Send a message to say that we are watching a suspicious craft to the north-west. It looks like a British submarine. If we start our engines it might hear us. That will account for the delay and give us plenty of time to slip away.'

Li Chi went to the bridge and made the signal. Biggles went with him.

'Now advise Tamashoa to warn all ships in the vicinity to be on the look out for a British Submarine,' he requested as an afterthought.

'With what object?' queried Li Chi, a suspicion of surprise creeping into his voice.

'That should set the destroyers on a new course, out of our way,' explained Biggles. 'Besides, I've got the glimmering of an idea.'

'Always you have an idea,' murmured Li Chi.

'Ideas sometimes win battles—when they come off,' returned Biggles, smiling faintly.

Li Chi sent the signal, which was acknowledged.

'Okay. Let's go,' said Biggles, and returned to the deck. Li Chi remained on the bridge. A bell tinkled somewhere below. The *Sumatran's* deck vibrated slightly as the engines were started. Water boiled astern as the ship's bows swung round towards Elephant Island. The *Lotus* followed.

# Chapter 12
# How Algy Ditched The Gosling

Apart from the gruelling monotony of the passage, Algy's flight to India was uneventful. Putting down his wheels he landed at the service aerodrome at Madras, where he was quickly surrounded by members of the squadron who demanded in no uncertain terms to be told how much longer they were to be kept waiting. They were browned off in every sense of the word, asserted Angus Mackail, who was flying again, although he still showed signs of wear and tear, the result—as he put it—of his 'crumper' in Burma some months ago.*

Over a quick lunch Algy passed on Biggles' orders, then went to station headquarters to carry out the other duties assigned to him. These occupied him for some time. He saw the two Lightnings take off and head eastward but nearly two hours elapsed before he was able to follow.

'We shall expect you sometime tomorrow morning,' he told those who were to fly the transport Liberators. 'Don't forget to bring some juice—we shall need it.'

For the first five hours his return trip was as devoid of incident as the outward journey. He flew through a

* His crash—See Biggles in the Orient, published by Red Fox

world of sea and sky—and nothing else. From his altitude of five thousand feet the Indian Ocean lay as flat as a tropic sea can be in its most placid mood. Always lonely, on the course he took to pass between the Andaman and Nicobar Islands, war appeared to have swept the sea clean. The sky was a mighty dome of blue, steely-ultramarine overhead, fading to pale azure at the horizon which, seeming to rise to his own level, created an impression that he was flying from rim to rim across a colossal basin.

Not for five hours did any mark, large or small, break the pristine purity of the azure world through which he flew; then his ever-questioning eyes came to rest on a smudge of smoke on the northern horizon, so faint that had there been anything else to arrest the eye it might have passed unnoticed. The smoke could mean the presence of only one thing—a ship. It might be a friend or it might be a foe. He was taking no chances, so he turned slightly to the south to keep well clear. Automatically he scanned the sky ahead of him along his new course, and again, almost at once, his eyes came to rest, this time on two tiny specks, no larger than midges, that moved at about his own height in a northerly direction across the vault of implacable blue. Obviously, they were aircraft, and although they were still too far off for identification he knew it was unlikely that they would be British. All he could do was turn away in the hope, a remote hope, that he would not be seen. There was no question of taking cover, for in all the vast expanse of sea and sky that surrounded him there was nothing that could have hidden a fly. He felt—and, indeed, he was—as conspicuous as a bumble bee in a whitewashed cell.

His hopes of escaping observation did not last long. He knew, from the way the two machines turned sharply, the moment the pilots saw him. And there was still nothing he could do. He had not enough petrol to take him back to India even if he had so wished. If he turned he would soon be overtaken, as he swiftly perceived, for his companions in space were now close enough for recognition. He made them out to be a pair of Mitsubishi ship fighters. And he was not equipped for fighting. The situation was all fairly clear. The smudge on the northern horizon, he reasoned, was a Japanese aircraft carrier. The two Mitsubishis had been out on reconnaissance and were returning to their parent ship. He had cut across their course at an unfortunate moment. It was bad luck, but that risk was always present. He was well aware of it. Biggles had known it when he had made his arrangements, but as he had said at the time, they could not carry fighting equipment if they were to load enough petrol for a trans-ocean flight.

Algy knew, as they say in India, that his time had come.

He took the only course open to him. Flying now on full throttle he dived steeply, back on his original course for Elephant Island, still nearly four hundred miles away. He reckoned he had one chance. If the Mitsubishis had made a long reconnaissance they might be short of petrol; they might have left themselves only enough to return to the ship with a slight margin. If that was so they would not be able to follow him far, if by taking evading action he could avoid their early attacks.

The Mitsubishis quickly overtook him, as he knew

they would. By the time they were within range he was down to fifty feet, racing just above the surface of the placid sea. This low altitude would to some extent worry the fighters in that they would not be able to press their attack too close for fear of overshooting their mark and colliding with the water. Algy flew with his eyes on the reflector, watching the two Mitsubishis, which had remained together and were coming down behind him—the orthodox tactics for such an attack. He knew just when they would fire, and was ready. He slammed the control column over and skidded out of the line of bullets. This happened three times, and he did not suppose that he would be allowed to get away with such a simple manoeuvre a fourth time. He was right. The two fighters parted company and attacked together from either side. Several bullets struck the Gosling but without in any way affecting its perform-ance. Nevertheless, Algy was far from happy. Apart from the petrol in his tanks he was carrying fifteen four-gallon cans. He was, in fact, a flying petrol tank. And the Japs were using tracer.* One bullet in the right place would be enough to cause the Gosling to explode like a bomb.

His hopes flared up when one of the fighters now turned away and headed north. That could only mean that it was short of fuel. But his hopes were dashed when the remaining fighter, in what seemed to be a final effort—and the attack was pressed closely on that account—came right in. Algy did everything he knew, but it seemed that the Gosling's controls had been hit,

* Phosphoros-loaded bullets whose course through the air can be seen by day or night

for the machine responded sluggishly to his frantic efforts with control column and rudder bar.* The port engine coughed. The needle of the revolution indicator swung back. Grey petrol vapour swirled aft. With a swift flick of his hand Algy switched off. The Gosling, loaded to capacity, sank bodily. Algy tried to hold the machine off, but the controls were sticky and it only half responded. Two seconds later the aircraft struck the water with a mighty splash, bounced, splashed again, and then came to rest, rocking.

Algy threw a swift glance over his shoulder, saw the Mitsubishi coming at him in a businesslike way, so he went overboard, taking such cover as the airframe could provide. He heard, rather than saw, the result of the enemy machine's final burst. There was a noise such as a tree makes in falling. It lasted less than three seconds. Then the sound ended abruptly. The drone of the engine began to recede.

Climbing up out of the water Algy saw the fighter turning towards the north at the top of its zoom. For a minute he watched it, prepared for it to come back; but when it held on after its companion he made a quick inspection of the aircraft, which apart from a considerable number of holes appeared to have suffered no serious damage. The great thing was—and in this respect he realised he had been lucky—the machine had not taken fire. Dripping water, he climbed on the centre-section and sat down to consider his position; and it did not take him long to conclude that it was not very bright. He was more than three hundred miles

* Foot-operated lever which the pilot uses to control the direction of flight

117

from the nearest land—the Mergui Archipelago. The chances of getting the machine airworthy were too small to be considered seriously. But—and this was the factor that set him hoping again—he was not far off the direct course from Madras to Elephant Island. If the sea remained calm, and if the aircraft did not sink—and bearing in mind the five watertight compartments in the hull he did not think they could all be holed—there was a good chance that one of the Liberators would spot him on its outward run to the island the following day. It would not be able to pick him up, but Biggles would at least know where he was. Curiously enough, the possibility of what did actually happen did not occur to him. The last thing he thought of was that he might be picked up by a ship; and for this reason his astonishment knew no bounds when, just as dusk was closing in, he saw not one but six columns of black smoke appear above the northern horizon. Six hulls, which he soon made out to be six destroyers, appeared under the smoke. They were, he observed, making directly towards him; and with a sinking feeling in the stomach he knew why. There was nothing remarkable about it. The two Mitsubishis would be certain to report their combat. They would report that the aircraft was still afloat. Obviously enemy ships in the vicinity would be sent to the spot.

The destroyers, flying the Rising Sun of Japan,* their decks lined with curious faces, came close. One moved alongside. A rope was thrown. Algy took it and was hauled aboard. An officer dropped down to the Gosling, searched it and returned. The destroyer backed away.

* National flag of Japan, a red sun on a white background

A gun fired three shots. The Gosling went up in a sheet of flame. Algy was allowed to watch this with an armed escort standing beside him. Then he was marched below, to a cabin in which behind a desk sat an officer of senior rank-judging by the amount of gold braid he carried. Two junior officers stood behind him. At a small table sat a clerk with a writing pad before him. Algy was searched, everything in his pockets being piled on the table. The senior officer examined everything carefully. This formality over, at a word from him, one of the juniors, who apparently had been appointed to act as interpreter, addressed Algy with a curious sing song intonation.

'You are to tell your name, service and rank,' said he.

Algy gave this information.

'Where are you from?' was the next question.

'I have nothing more to say,' answered Algy.

'It will be better for you if you talk freely,' promised the officer.

'I know, but I prefer to say nothing,' returned Algy.

Upon this there was a brief conversation between the interpreter and the senior officer.

Addressing Algy again the interpreter inquired, 'Where do you go and why do you carry petrol?'

'I have already told you that I have nothing more to say,' answered Algy. 'In that, as you know quite well, I am within my rights as a prisoner of war.'

There was another conversation in Japanese.

'It will be bad for you if you do not answer questions,' said the interpreter.

Algy nodded. 'I know.'

'You will say nothing?'

'Nothing. I have told you all that I am compelled to tell you.'

'You will be sorry.'

'No,' stated Algy. 'Whatever you do I shall not be sorry.'

That ended the interview. The escort took charge of the prisoner who was marched out to end a short journey in a small bare cell somewhere in the bottom of the ship. He was locked in. There was no porthole, but light was provided by a small electric bulb behind a grill. There was a bunk. Algy lay on it and gave himself up to the contemplation of his position. Most of his thoughts were naturally of a speculative nature. He wondered where the ship would take him—Singapore, Rangoon, Penang, Japan . . . it might be anywhere. The flotilla might be at sea for days, perhaps for weeks. He wondered how Biggles would manage without the Gosling and what he would think about its non-return. He wondered if the squadron would ever know what happened to him . . . and so on.

Time passed. It seemed a long time. Algy did not know how long for his watch had been taken from him. He only knew that it must now be night. It was hot, stuffy, in the cabin. No one came near him. After a while he fell asleep.

# Chapter 13
# Algy Meets A Friend—and an Enemy

Algy was tired, and for this reason he slept long and heavily, as he realised in a vague sort of way when he was awakened by a steward who brought a dish of rice mixed with some sort of fish. The escort watched from the door.

'What time is it?' asked Algy.

The steward made signs which Algy took to mean that he did not understand; he did not pursue the matter and the man went out, the escort locking the door behind him.

Another long weary period elapsed before it was opened again. This time the officer-interpreter was with the escort. He ordered Algy to follow.

'You go on shore now,' said he. 'Perhaps now you will speak,' he added, with something like a sneer.

'I don't think so,' replied Algy evenly.

'Perhaps Admiral Tamashoa make you change your mind,' said the Jap coldly.

That was the first indication Algy had that the destroyer had arrived at Victoria Point. Nearing the deck he saw that it was broad daylight. The destroyers were dropping anchor at what at first appeared to be a land-locked lagoon. Algy had never seen the place before but he supposed it to be the estuary of the Pak

Chan River. It was a depressing looking place. On all sides the forest dropped sheer into the sea. A muddy foreshore, on which lay a few dilapidated *prahus* was backed by a street of houses, mostly ramshackle. A wooden landing stage—it could hardly be called a pier—thrust its rotting timbers out into the stagnant water. A line of decomposing vegetation followed the high water mark. There was nothing Eastern about the place. So this, thought Algy, was the place Tamashoa had made his headquarters.

Still under escort he was taken ashore in a boat lowered for the purpose, and at the landing stage was handed over to a squad of Japanese soldiers, who took him to what he learned later had been the bungalow of the District Police Superintendent. There were a lot of Japanese troops about, mostly undersized little men dressed in the shoddiest of uniforms. It struck him there was as good deal of activity, although what it was about he did not know.

He finished his short march in what had obviously been the local jail, a little square cell on the edge of an open space behind the bungalow. A small barred window let in a little air, but the place was in a filthy condition and stank abominably. But he paid little attention to such details, for to his astonishment the cell was already occupied, and by a white man. Dressed in a flannel suit, torn and stained with blood, this man sat on the floor trying to bandage a wound in his leg with a piece of old newspaper. Staring at the man Algy was pushed inside. The door slammed. A key turned in the lock.

'Good day to you, sir,' said the wounded man, looking up from his task. 'Forgive my not rising, but I'm

122

having a little trouble with my leg. One of the devils stuck a bayonet into it. Damn scoundrel. I was already a prisoner. But allow me to introduce myself. My name is Marling, one time major in His Majesty's Indian Army.'

'I've heard of you,' said Algy. 'My name's Lacey, Flight Lieutenant, Royal Air Force. A friend of mine has just been to . . .' Algy glanced round and dropped his voice. 'I'm a friend of Bigglesworth,' he went on tersely. 'What are you doing here? What has happened at Shansie? Excuse me, sir, but that paper isn't much use. I can fix a better bandage than that.' Without any messing about Algy ripped a sleeve out of his shirt.

'Thanks. That's most kind of you,' said Marling. 'Shansie, I'm afraid, is finished. Bigglesworth was right. 'Fraid I was a bit too confident. Still, I did what I could.'

'What happened?' asked Algy, working on the wound.

'The morning after Bigglesworth went, a Jap plane came flying over—looking for the *Lotus* I imagine. We were at work making an aerodrome. If you've seen Bigglesworth he will have told you about it. The Jap must have guessed what we were up to. Next thing we knew Japs were dropping on us out of the sky. Paratroops, I believe they call 'em. Well, there we were. We had a little affair that lasted about twenty minutes or so, then they caught me.'

'What happened to your son?'

'Wish I knew. Lost sight of him in the scuffle. Last I saw of him was using a *parang* with one of my fellows named Melong. Of course, they might have got into the forest.'

123

This information worried Algy not a little. 'Then the Japanese have taken over Shansie?' he queried.

'Without a doubt.'

'In that case Biggles—that is, Squadron Leader Bigglesworth—may step into a trap if he goes there to see you.'

''Fraid you're right, my boy. Can't do anything about it though, can we?'

'It looks that way, I must admit. Why did the Japanese bayonet you?'

'Wanted me to tell 'em where I'd hidden my rubber and my rubies.'

'You didn't tell them?'

'Tell them? No fear. Won't get a word out of me, blast them. I've had a set to with this fellow Tamashoa. He didn't get anything out of me, either. I told him what I thought of him. How did they get hold of you?'

Algy gave a brief account of his misfortune.

'Bad luck. Damn bad luck. Tamashoa will be seeing you. Won't get anything out of you though, I'll bet.'

'Not a word.'

'That's the spirit. Don't talk to the scum.'

'Have you any idea of the time, sir?' asked Algy as he finished the bandage.

'Sun's going down—must be nearly six o'clock. Soon be dark. Devil of a place to pass the night. Place stinks.'

At this point the door was opened and a Japanese non-commissioned officer appeared, behind him an escort of four soldiers with bayonets fixed. He beckoned to the prisoners in turn.

'I suppose he means we're to go with them,' said Algy. 'You'd better not move with that leg, sir, or you'll start it bleeding again.' He tried to point this out to the N.C.O.,* and he may have succeeded; but if he did the only effect it had on the Japanese was to cause him to cross the cell and drag the major roughly to his feet.

Algy started forward, his face flaming resentment; but Marling spoke to him sharply. 'Steady, my boy, or they'll stick a bayonet into you, too. I can manage.'

The prisoners—Marling limping, with a hand on Algy's shoulder—had not far to go. They were marched to the front door of the bungalow where a sentry stood on duty. As they entered, a small party emerged, obviously another prisoner with an escort. The prisoner in this case was a Burmese youth. With the escort there was a burly Japanese, stripped to the waist, carrying a drawn sword—a heavy curved weapon.

As the two parties passed, Marling spoke to the prisoner, who answered, '*Baik, tuan.*'**

'That was Tapil, Melong's eldest son,' Marling told Algy. 'Apparently they caught the lad. Tamashoa has been trying to get him to talk.'

'What was that fellow doing with the drawn sword?' asked Algy.

'You'll probably find that out soon enough, my boy,' answered the major.

The party came to a halt outside a door. The N.C.O. knocked and went in. He came back and motioned the prisoners forward. Prisoners and escort went in.

Seated at a desk was the man Algy supposed to be Tamashoa. Several members of his staff stood behind him in attitudes of respectful attention. He was not what Algy expected. He thought to see a man of a

---

* Non-commissioned officer e.g. a corporal or a sergeant
** 'Very good, sir'

size and general appearance in proportion to his rank, instead of which the admiral was a smooth-faced, foppish-looking little man of barely middle age, absurdly over-dressed by European standards. His uniform was as impressive as that of a cinema attendant. The breast was hung with medals and studded with orders. When the prisoners entered he was reading a document—or for effect, making a pretence of doing so. This he continued to do for a full two minutes, during which a silence, embarrassing in its intensity, persisted. At length Tamashoa deigned to look up. He laid the paper aside and with his elbows on the desk looked at Algy.

'Answer questions,' he said, in fair English. 'What were you doing in airplane?'

'Flying,' answered Algy.

Tamashoa appeared to see nothing facetious in this answer. Not a muscle of his face moved. 'Quite so. What were you doing in sea?' he asked.

'Swimming,' replied Algy.

'Quite so. I mean, what are you doing here?' queried Tamashoa.

'Standing,' replied Algy evenly. He did not smile.

'Why?' asked Tamashoa.

'Because no one has offered me a seat.'

To Algy's astonishment, at a movement from the admiral a chair was brought and he was invited to sit. He gave the chair to the major, whereupon another chair was brought.

'You see we understand the courtesy,' said Tamashoa smoothly. 'Why did you carry petrol?'

'Because a plane needs petrol to fly.'

'Quite so. You are at Elephant Island?' asserted Tamashoa, getting his tenses mixed.

126

'No, I'm here,' corrected Algy.

'Quite so. Why are you at Elephant Island?'

'I'm not at Elephant Island,' asserted Algy, truthfully.

'There are British officers at Elephant Island.'

'Are there?'

'Why?'

'You tell me.'

At this juncture it appeared to occur to Tamashoa that he was not getting anywhere, although he could not understand why. The expressions on the faces of his staff did not change. They stood stock still, like dummy figures.

Tamashoa's next question showed an unbelievable lack of understanding of the Anglo-Saxon mind. 'If you will tell me why you were flying, and why British are on Elephant Island with the pirate Li Chi, you shall have your life.'

Algy shook his head. 'Has no one ever told you that we do not buy our lives from our enemies?'

'You will not tell me?'

'I will tell you nothing,' said Algy shortly.

'Quite so,' said Tamashoa. He turned to the major. 'Because I am by nature a man of great culture I shall give you another chance to tell me where you put the rubber and rubies of Shansie.'

'And because I am by nature an obstinate man I shall not tell you,' answered the major frostily.

Tamashoa said something in Japanese to the N.C.O. He tapped the prisoners on the shoulder and pointed to the window. Understanding that they were to look out Algy went across, as did Marling. The window overlooked the open area behind the bungalow. In it, in the light of a torch, a grim drama was being enacted. Melong's son was there. His hands had been tied behind his back. He was kneeling. Beside him stood the man with the sword.

Tamashoa joined the others at the window. 'Observe what happens to prisoners who are obstinate,' he said blandly. 'This man would not speak. If he will not speak he need not live. Soon, unless you can speak, you also will lose your heads.'

The executioner raised his sword. Algy watched the beginning of the downward stroke and turned away.

'Ah,' said Tamashoa. 'A pretty cut.'

'Scum,' said Marling in a thin, dry voice. 'Scum— that's what they are.'

'Does that help you to find your tongues?' queried Tamashoa.

'No,' answered Algy and the major together.

'Quite so,' said Tamashoa smoothly. He made a theatrical gesture to the escort and returned to his desk.

The escort closed in and the prisoners were marched out. On the front doorstep the man with the drawn sword was waiting. The N.C.O. spoke to him and he joined the party.

'I'm sorry about this,' Algy told the major. 'Now that I know what these skunks are really like I'd like to have one last crack at them.'

'I'm afraid you've left it a bit late, my boy,' said Major Marling, without emotion.

# Chapter 14
# Enter the Liberators

During the twenty-four hours Algy had been a prisoner Biggles had not been idle. Many things had happened on Elephant Island. The *Sumatran* had been captured and taken according to plan to the cove wherein the *Lotus* lay, where the work of loading her with rubber had begun forthwith, more than a hundred sweating men toiling, not as paid workmen, but as men who derive the utmost satisfaction from what they are doing. As nothing more could be done in this respect Biggles turned his attention to the new state of affairs brought about by the capture of Algy and the loss of the Gosling.

'I don't quite know what's going to happen here, but I have a feeling that things are working up for an almighty flap,' he told the others. 'What we've done has been more or less forced upon us; but it would be silly to suppose that Tamashoa is going to take the loss of two ships lying down. If he has to report the loss to his High Command it will mean considerable loss of face, and loss of face to a Japanese is worse than death. We shall have to try to do something about Algy. We've got to get the Liberators on the move. We've got to have petrol and we need another marine aircraft. I hope Li Chi will take the *Sumatran* to India as planned, but without an amphibian there can be no question of picking him up. He'll have to go all the way and come back in one of the Liberators later on. We've just about enough petrol to get one of the Lightnings to India, so I'd like you, Taffy, to push across right away. Get an amphibian from somewhere. If you can't get a Gosling get something else. One of the boys will have to bring it over right away. The Liberators had better start, too, right away, leaving at half hour intervals, as things stand the sooner they leave the better. The first machine will load up with petrol. The second will bring half a dozen H.E.* bombs—mix 'em up, but I want at least a couple of five hundred pounders.'

The others looked surprised. 'Did you say bombs?' queried Ginger.

'That's what I said.'

'What do you want bombs for?'

'I'm not quite sure, but with these destroyers in the offing they may be useful. Machine-gun bullets are no use against armour plate.'

'You want me to start for India right now?' asked Taffy.

'This minute. I'm worried about petrol. I was relying on Algy for some. An attack now would catch us on one leg.'

'In that case I'll push along,' said Taffy, and departed.

Biggles turned to Ferocity. 'Fill up the other Lightning with what drop of petrol we have left. Take off just before dawn and take care of things upstairs for as long as your petrol lasts. We can't have enemy machines about while the *Sumatran* is loading. We must give her every chance to get away. I don't know exactly when that will be—soon after daybreak I hope. Now

* High explosive

130

everyone had better get to bed. We look like having a busy day tomorrow'

'With Henry bringing a Gosling there will only be Angus, Tex and Tug, to handle Liberators,' Ginger pointed out.

'When Taffy tells them how urgent things are I reckon they'll bring one each,' said Biggles. 'That will be three, anyway. I shall send them straight back with anyone we can spare. I was hoping we should be able to operate with two pilots aboard each machine, but at the rate things are going we look like being lucky if we can operate five aircraft with one pilot in each. It's going to be hard work. I may decide to keep one Liberator here.'

'Why?'

'So that we can all get out if the whole thing comes unstuck. I hope you realise that at this moment we have one machine here, a Lightning, with enough petrol for less than half an hour's flying. That's bad. I suppose I should have made allowance for the Gosling getting ditched, but one can't think of everything. Poor old Algy.'

'What are we going to do about him?'

'We can't do anything while he's at sea in an enemy destroyer,' returned Biggles moodily. 'We shall know when he arrives at Victoria Point because I shall borrow Li Chi's glasses and keep watch across the strait from the top of the hill.'

'What are you going to do now, old boy?' asked Bertie.

'I'm going down to the cove to speak to Li Chi,' answered Biggles. 'You get some sleep.'

He found Li Chi watching the loading of the rubber

into the *Sumatran*. A human chain had been formed and the bundles, weighing a hundredweight or more apiece, were being manhandled from hand to hand. Ayert kept things on the move.

'Tell me this,' said Biggles to Li Chi. 'The *Sumatran* you remember, was lying out in what you call the channel, waiting for high water to move in close?'

'Yes.'

'Does that mean that the water in the estuary is shallow?'

'Not only shallow, but full of shoals—silt brought down by the river. It is a dangerous place for a ship of any size.'

'How deep is the best part of the estuary at low water?'

'Nowhere more than two fathoms*—and it is necessary to know just where such places are. That is why ships stay out in the channel. Why do you ask this?'

'Just a minute—let me finish,' murmured Biggles. 'The estuary, I take it, is fed by the Pak Chan?'

'Yes.'

'If the water in the river fell suddenly there would be a big drop at the estuary?'

'Naturally. But the river is not likely to dry up at this time of the year.'

'That's where you're wrong,' declared Biggles. 'It is. I'm going to make it.'

'You are having trouble with your intestines again my friend,' said Li Chi sadly. 'In any case, how would the drying up of the river help us?'

'The destroyers are on their way to Victoria Point.'

* Approximately three metres

'They will anchor in the channel.'

'They may, but I don't think they will. They will have been warned that a British submarine is about. What would you do in that case, if you were in command of the flotilla?'

'If I was not to be at the place for very long I should risk the mud and get into the estuary under cover of the shore batteries.'*

'Exactly. Do you remember what Major Marling said about floods, and how he had to dam the river to keep it in its bed? Suppose that dam, or embankment, or whatever it is, was broken down. The water would spill itself over the landscape wouldn't it? Not much would come down the river. The result would be a sudden drop, a big drop, at the estuary.'

Li Chi drew a deep breath. 'What happiness!' he exclaimed. 'The destroyers would find themselves stuck on the mud. At that disadvantage you will attack them?'

'Not on your life. My intestines would be very much out of order if they induced me to do anything as silly as that,' returned Biggles. 'This is the point. The sailors would not be able to cross the mud to get ashore if there was trouble there, and if the ships heeled over, as they might, they would find it difficult, if not impossible, to use their guns.'

'You don't want the sailors to go ashore?'

'I don't want them to be able to get ashore in force.'

'Why?'

'Because I myself shall be at Victoria Point tonight with volunteers for a commando raid.'

* Artillery and anti-aircraft guns

133

'To prevent an invasion of Elephant Island!'

'Partly. But you seem to forget that a friend of ours will soon be at Victoria Point, a prisoner of war. We must get him away—or try. There is no telling what Tamashoa will do to him when he refuses to co-operate.'

'This is plain war,' said Li Chi. 'What about the rubber?'

'I haven't forgotten it. The arrangements for its shipment still stand.'

'But how will you get the embankment at Shansie broken down? It will mean a visit to Major Marling.'

'I, or someone, will have to fly to Shansie as soon as a machine is available. That should be sometime tomorrow.'

'Do you want me to go?'

'No. You'll be at sea in the *Sumatran*—that is, if you are still prepared to go through with it. I'm afraid it will mean going all the way to India, but one of my boys will bring you back in a Liberator.'

'The only thing is, if I go how will you talk to my men? They do not speak English.'

'Ayert does. I want you to leave him here with me, to act as interpreter.'

Li Chi thought for a moment. 'We have always sailed together,' he murmured. 'Still, no doubt he will stay if I ask him.'

'How long will it take to get the ship loaded?' was Biggles' next question. 'Is there any possibility of getting away by dawn?'

'It might be done if we stopped at a thousand tons,' answered Li Chi thoughtfully. 'But as the sea is dead calm and should remain so for some time now until the monsoon breaks, I am thinking of taking a deck cargo—perhaps a hundred tons. If we strike heavy weather it would of course have to go overboard. The only thing against it is the delay in getting the ship away.'

'It's worth the risk,' decided Biggles. 'I shouldn't have thought of it.' He smiled. 'That's the best of having a sailor around. Get away as soon as you can. You know the danger. I'm going to snatch some sleep—you'd better do the same.'

'My friend, five thousand years ago the Chinese taught themselves to do without sleep for long periods,' said Li Chi placidly. 'When I was a boy my father made me sit and stare at my great toe for twenty-four hours at a time without moving. That is Chinese training.'

Biggles laughed. 'If my father had caught me doing that he would have sent for the doctor.' He returned to the bungalow and without taking off his clothes threw himself on a divan.

He was awakened by the roar of an aircraft, and recognising the voice of the Lightning he hurried out. It was still dark but the stars were paling in the sky. Presently Bertie came in to say that Ferocity had taken off for his dawn patrol. It was nearly six o'clock. Feeling better for the rest Biggles had a bath and felt even better. He had, he knew, a hectic anxious day in front of him. The runway was not so complete as he would have liked for the Liberators, but his hand was being forced. Ginger appeared, yawning. Li Chi's cook brought tea, and soon afterwards Li Chi came in to say that the *Sumatran* would be ready for sea in an hour.

'Don't forget to fly a British flag or you may find

yourself in a spot of trouble with one of our submarines or destroyers,' warned Biggles.

'I have spent most of my life dodging the British navy,' said Li Chi, with one of his rare smiles. 'Now I should be glad to see it.'

For the moment nothing more could be done. The atmosphere was one of expectancy, due partly to the distant drone of Ferocity's Lightning high overhead. After breakfast they all went down to the *Sumatran* where the natives were still toiling.

'I have told Ayert to stay and take orders from you while I am away,' said Li Chi to Biggles.

Beyond the Isthmus of Malaya, dawn had now broken, flooding the smooth water with pink, gold, and the translucent hues of mother-of-pearl. And with it came a growing sound that justified Biggles' precaution of putting up the Lightning on a defensive patrol.

'There he is!' exclaimed Ginger, pointing at a speck of light that was speeding across the sky from the mainland towards the island.

Biggles shaded his eyes. 'Kawanishi 94 . . . single-engined three-seater navy type reconnaissance sea-plane,' he murmured. 'Ferocity should be able to handle him.'

They watched. There was no sign of the Lightning for it was too high to be seen, and the drone of the lower Kawanishi now drowned the purr of its engine. But this state of affairs did not last long. This time it was Bertie who pointed. A tiny speck was falling diagonally out of the sky towards the Japanese aircraft. 'Here comes Ferocity,' he said, adjusting his eyeglass. 'I should say he's got a sitter.'

Faintly to the ears of the listeners came the long

drawn out howl of the diving fighter. The Kawanishi came straight on in level flight, a clear indication that the machine above it had not been seen. It is likely that the attentions of the crew, as Biggles had predicted, were concentrated on the scene below without a thought of danger.

'Ferocity's taking a chance with the rear gunner,' observed Ginger critically, as the Lightning, now clearly revealed, came on down in a steep curving dive that brought it behind the enemy aircraft.

'He can probably see what the rear gunner's doing— we can't,' said Biggles.

The combat, if combat it could be called, lasted about five seconds. The Lightning went in close before it opened fire. There was no return fire from the enemy machine. Tracer streaked. A few pieces fell off the Kawanishi. There was a short burst of fire from the rear gun, but the tracer went so wide of its mark that it was evident the gunner had fired in desperate haste. No second opportunity was afforded him to correct his error. The Kawanishi's tanks exploded and the machine began to fall, a ball of fire, towards the sea.

'No time to use their brollies,'* murmured Bertie. 'The doctor won't be able to do anything for *them*, by Jove!'

'Take a lesson from it,' advised Biggles. 'Wherever you are, never take it for granted that you've got the sky to yourself.'

The Kawanishi fell into the sea about a mile from the nearest point of the island, leaving a long blank plume of smoke to mark its passing. A cheer went

* Slang: parachutes

up from the natives who had paused in their work of loading.

Ferocity landed and taxied quickly to the shelter. The others went along.

'Nice work, Ferocity,' congratulated Biggles.

'I thought I'd better come in—juice is running low,' said Ferocity casually.

'Quite right. It's ten to one the Japanese will wait for their machine to come back before sending out another. That will give us breathing space. You'd better stand by though—in case. The first Liberator should be along presently with some petrol.'

An hour later, with no danger threatening, the *Sumatran* steamed out of the cove with Li Chi on the bridge, a grinning, dirty but picturesque crew lining the rail, and more than a hundred tons of deck cargo giving her an untidy, top-heavy appearance. Li Chi took a course, on Biggles' advice, south of west, to avoid any chance of running into the enemy destroyers. While those ashore stood watching—Biggles with a good deal of anxiety, for the ship looked as helpless as a maimed sheep—a Lightning appeared in the western sky, flying low and flat out. It landed and Taffy leaned out. He waved and climbed down. His face was set in hard lines from the strain of his double flight; his chin was unshaven and the corners of his eyes were bloodshot. He swayed slightly on his feet as he made his report. It amounted to this. A Gosling was being sent up from Ceylon to Madras. Henry Harcourt was waiting for it and would bring it across as soon as it arrived. Three Liberators were coming out—as many machines as there were pilots available. He had pushed on ahead of them. 'By the way,' he concluded, 'I noticed a lot of smoke away up to the north about ten minutes ago, look you. I kept clear of it.'

'That'll be the destroyers,' said Biggles. 'Grab some breakfast and have a rest while you can.'

There were now two Lightnings on the island but the fuel was low in the tanks of both. This, however, was remedied when half an hour later the first Liberator arrived. Markers were put out for it. For Biggles, who stood watching, the actual landing was a brief period of acute suspense, for as yet there had been no proof that the runway would stand up to the strain imposed on it by an aircraft of the weight of a Liberator. The timber landing area sagged a little, that was all, and he drew a deep breath of relief when the powerful wheel brakes came into action to pull the machine up with a fair margin of safety. He hurried down to greet the pilot, the others following. It was Angus. He climbed up beside him and directed him to the shelter.

'I'm carrying a load of petrol,' announced Angus. 'Tex and Tug are following me,' he went on, as they climbed down, Angus buffeting himself to restore circulation. 'No doot Taffy told ye about Henry waiting for the Gosling? That leaves two Liberators at Madras waiting for pilots. I'm sorry aboot Algy. Taffy told us.'

Biggles nodded. 'It'll make us short handed. I must have been crazy to think that ten of us could handle a job of this size. I didn't allow for casualties. Still, having started, we shall have to go on. Sorry, Angus, but I'm afraid you'll have to go straight back. It isn't only a matter of getting a load of rubber across; we've got to get the others across so that we can start operating at full strength. Ginger will stay here with me. Now we're all right for petrol we'll handle the Lightnings — should it become necessary. But we'd better get the petrol unloaded; we may need it any time now. Ferocity shot down a Kawanishi a little while ago and I fancy the enemy will soon be sending another machine over to look for it.'

The petrol which the Liberator had brought was unloaded and dumped and the tanks of the two Lightnings were filled, these tasks occupying some time. Hardly were they finished when a drone in the west announced the arrival of another Liberator. They all stood waiting while the machine came in. Suddenly Biggles swung round and stared towards the east.

'Confound it!' he snapped. 'Just what I didn't want to happen.' He pointed at a speck in the sky that was moving towards the island from the mainland. 'If that Jap sees the Liberator land our game will soon be up,' he went on tersely. 'He mustn't see it. I'll go after him. Ginger, take the other Lightning and get out over the strait in case he dodges me.'

The two Lightnings took off one behind the other. Biggles swung round in a steep climbing turn to the north. Ginger, holding his machine low, tore out across the strait for some distance before starting to climb. By now it was possible to identify the enemy plane as a Zero, flying at about ten thousand feet; but this time the pilot was wide awake and not to be caught. He must have seen the Lightnings—or one of them—for he turned suddenly and made for home, nose down. With plenty of height to spare Ginger realised that pursuit was futile—unless he followed the Zero to its base, which he felt sure was not Biggles' intention. He saw Biggles turning back towards the lake so he did the same thing. The Liberator was landing so they had to wait for it to get clear before they could get in. They found Tex O'Hara in the shelter.

'What goes on?' demanded Tex. 'You seem kinda busy.'

'We're a sight *too* busy,' answered Biggles. 'Instead of a quiet little hide-out this place is developing into a major airport. Did you notice a ship heading south-west as you came over—she'd be about twenty miles out?'

'Sure I saw her.'

'Was she all right?'

'I didn't notice anything wrong.'

'That's something, anyway,' murmured Biggles. 'She's carrying eleven hundred tons of rubber, which is so much less for us to lug across. Pity that Zero got away, but I don't think it saw very much. What have you brought, Tex?'

'Cookies. You asked for 'em. What in thunder do you want 'em for?'

'I just thought they might be handy. Let's get them down and out of the way. I want these machines out of the way, too. Angus, see about loading up with rubber. Taffy and Ferocity will go back with you. Same with you, Tex. You can take Bertie. Take turns at the stick and you'll get a rest. Ginger, slip along to Ayert and tell him to get his boys hauling the rubber.'

'What do we do when we get back to India?' asked Tex.

'Turn round and come back. You'll have to rest, of course, but don't waste time. Sorry to rush you, boys, but we've got to get the job going—and going fast. Once the Japs rumble what's happening here, and as far as they're concerned Elephant Island must be

141

beginning to stink, this place is going to be anything but a health resort.'

With the help of Ayert's men the bombs were unloaded and rubber was being packed into both machines when the next Liberator arrived, and landed, with Tug Carrington at the controls. There was no room for it in the shelter so it had to wait outside. Biggles stood and watched the eastern sky with a worried frown until Angus announced that he was ready. Biggles waved him away. With Angus went Taffy and Ferocity. Tug taxied in. Soon afterwards Tex went off, taking Bertie. Tug's Liberator was relieved of its burden of fuel and oil.

'Shall I ask Ayert to load her up with rubber?' asked Ginger.

Biggles sat on a log and mopped his face. 'Just a minute. I'm getting dizzy. Gosh! This is navvies' work. Let me think. How are you, Tug?'

Tug grinned. 'Right as rain. Want me to carry on after the others?'

'Not just yet,' decided Biggles. 'You know we've lost Algy and the Gosling? That leaves us only the two Lightnings, and I don't like being stuck here without sufficient transport to get us all away should things come unstuck. I think you'd better hang around for a bit and rest—anyway, until Harry arrives with the new Gosling. I ought to go and see Major Marling but with all this going on here I don't like leaving. Ginger, I think you'd better go to see Marling. Take one of the Lightnings. It'll be more likely to get you out of trouble if you run into any than the Gosling, even if you waited for it. Marling said he'd have a landing ground ready and I don't think he's the sort of chap to let us down.

142

Anyhow, if you can't find a place to land you'll have to come back.'

'Okay. Just what do you want me to tell him?'

'For a start, you'd better tell him about Algy, and these destroyers. I'm going to try to get Algy tonight. The destroyers will be in the estuary, I think. They'll turn their guns on us, to say nothing of putting sailors ashore if there is a rumpus—and there's likely to be one. I don't see how it can be avoided. Ask Marling to break down or blow up that embankment that keeps the water in the river. Soon after sundown would be the best time because that would give the destroyers plenty of time to get in. Explain to him that the idea is to get them aground on the mud. It may not work but we can try it.'

'Shall I go right away?' asked Ginger.

'You might as well. Keep clear of Victoria Point. Head north for a bit and then shoot straight across the jungle. Keep your eyes skinned for those destroyers; they must be getting close, and you don't want to have any truck with *them*. Come straight back after you've explained things to Marling. If I'm not here you'll find me on the hill watching for the destroyers through Li Chi's glasses. I shall have to see just where they go.'

'Shan't be long,' said Ginger, and walked down to his machine. In five minutes he was off, heading north preparatory to turning east.

Biggles spoke to Tug. 'You'd better get some sleep,' he advised. 'You'll find a bed in the bungalow. The cook will give you something to eat.'

'So you've decided to leave my machine where it is?'

'For the time being. She can't be seen from topsides.'

143

'I'm not really tired,' declared Tug. 'Sure there's nothing you'd like me to do?'

'Thanks, Tug. There's one thing you can do if you feel up to it.'

'What's that?'

'Take the spare Lightning and slip out and have a dekko at the *Sumatran*, to make sure she's all right. You should find her on a course just south of west, getting on for a hundred miles out. It would be a load off my mind to know that she's running out of the real danger zone.'

'It's as good as done,' said Tug, and walked off to the aircraft.

# Chapter 15
# Shocks for Biggles

After watching Tug take off, Biggles looked at his watch and saw that the time was after one o'clock. He realised that he was now the only one of the team left on the island.

For a little while he sat still, deep in thought. He had no appetite for food. His face, with one of those rare complexions that never seem to get sunburned, was beginning to show signs of the strain imposed by the fast-moving events of the last forty-eight hours. The strain, of course, fell on all, but the responsibility of leadership was his alone. He was driving his pilots hard and he knew it. They had not complained and probably never would complain, but he did not need telling that they would not be able to stand the present pace for very long. The sultry heat was enervating and did not make for clear thinking. Yet decisions, important decisions involving risk of life to others, would have to be made—had already been made, almost from hour to hour.

The thought of Algy a prisoner in enemy hands affected him far more than he was prepared to reveal to the others. Probably they felt the same. While he did not allow himself to dwell upon the possibility of Algy or Ginger becoming a casualty there was always a fear of it lurking in the background of his mind. If one of them went it would make a difference. The others would go on and the war would go on but things would not be the same. In war, duty, as defined by the High Command, made no allowance for personal feelings; they were supposed not to exist; and the British fighting forces in their many wars had established a sort of tradition in this respect. However a man might feel, it was considered weak to let others see any sort of emotion. The whole thing was of course a pose. Everyone who had fought an action knew it—commanding officers more than anyone, although the rank and file did not always realise it; did not suspect that behind the dispassionate voice giving orders that would send men to their deaths, a man's heart was being mauled. Perhaps it was a good thing. If men were going to break down every time a comrade failed to return, the will to win would soon break down. After it was all over—well, a man might let himself go. Alexander the Great had shut himself up in his tent for three days. Julius Caesar . . . Mark Antony . . . they had broken down and wept, and they were soldiers. Wellington had been unable to restrain his tears after Waterloo—and his troops called him the Iron Duke. Thus pondered Biggles, with gnawing anxiety in his heart, but with hardly a word of reference to Algy on his lips. His job was to get rubber, not indulge in private enterprises to satisfy personal feelings. Nevertheless, he mused, without comradeship a war would be hard to fight, and while he was not prepared to jeopardise his mission to save anyone, least of all himself, he was not prepared to let Algy go without making a desperate effort to save him.

He perceived clearly now the magnitude of the task he had undertaken. It had never looked easy even from

146

the start; but now, with unforeseen difficulties cropping up at every turn it began to look hopeless. He had not made the admission to the others but he had very little hope of getting all the rubber away. The enemy knew that a force led by British officers was on Elephant Island. Obviously, a man like Tamashoa would not allow it to remain there—right on his doorstep, so to speak. An attack in force could be expected almost any time. Even if a landing on Elephant Island was not made it seemed likely that enemy bombers would soon be in action; the opportunity for their employment was too plain to be overlooked. The destroyers, unless they were put out of action, would almost certainly shell the island.* Their arrival on the scene was an unexpected complication. The only bright spots that Biggles could see were the completion of the runway, which at least enabled him to operate, and the seizure of the *Sumatran*, which had cleared nearly a quarter of the rubber immediately available at one stroke.

Still thinking, with a movement that had become automatic he tapped the ash from his cigarette. Presently, with Li Chi's binoculars in his hand, he got up and walked to the end of the runway where he expected to find Ayert supervising its extension. The work was going on more slowly now that the logs at the water's edge had been used; but the men had worked hard and had done a good job. The men were still there, working, but Ayert was not with them. Biggles mentioned his name, whereupon the nearest workman pointed to the

---

* Use their heavy calibre guns to bombard the island with high explosive shells.

shore. Ayert was there, talking with an almost naked coolie.

Biggles turned to go across to him, but before reaching the spot, he heard Tug coming back, so he waited for the Lightning to land to hear what he had to say. His nerves tightened when he saw the expression on Tug's face. He ran the last few yards.

'Sorry, chief, but I'm afraid it's bad news,' said Tug apologetically, as if it were his fault.

'Go on,' ordered Biggles tersely.

'The Japs have collected the *Sumatran*—or it looks like it,' said Tug. 'She's stopped, with another ship, a bigger ship, drawing up to her. It was hard to see exactly what was happening and I didn't like to go too close in case they opened up on me.... I thought I'd better come straight back to let you know.'

'Thanks, Tug,' said Biggles quietly. 'It's a nasty crack, but we did all we could. I suppose we were hoping for a lot, to think she might get away. I'd better stick to planes in future. You go and get some rest while you can. Ginger should be back any time now.'

Tug taxied on to the shelter while Biggles went across to Ayert, whom he imagined was talking to one of Li Chi's spies that arrived from the mainland from time to time. The bosun saw him coming and walked to meet him.

'Bad,' said Ayert. 'Velly much bad.'

'What's bad?' asked Biggles.

'Shansie finish. Marling *tuan* gone. Lalla gone. All gone. All finish. Japs take. Japs stay.'

Biggles steadied himself. This second blow, coming right on top of the one Tug had just given him, was hard to take. 'How do you know this?' he asked Ayert.

148

'Man come. He speak.'

'What man?'

'Spy man from Victoria Point. He swim out in old canoe to north side of island then come walking. Man say Japs all talking. Say Shansie finish.'

'And the Japs are still there?'

'Yes, *tuan*. Japs there. Planes—many planes.'

'I wish I'd known this half an hour ago,' muttered Biggles. He was thinking of Ginger. 'Thanks for the information, Ayert. Thank that man for coming. Good work.'

Ayert grinned. It was clear that as far as he was concerned this was all part of the day's work.

But Biggles did not smile. The situation was too serious, and seemed to be deteriorating, as the official bulletins put it, faster than he could cope with it. Ginger had gone to Shansie and there was nothing he could do about it. However, it did not seem sufficient reason for abandoning his plan. On the contrary, there was now all the more reason why he should go on with it. He asked Ayert if he would go with him to the top of the hill to watch for the destroyers. Ayert, who knew every inch of the water, would be able to tell him what might not be apparent through the glasses. The big bosun acquiesced readily, and they were walking towards the track that led up the hill when the roar of an aircraft flying flat out brought Biggles round, staring, hoping. His face lit up when a Lightning came skimming over the treetops to make a quick, rather risky landing on the runway. Biggles dashed down to intercept it. As he drew near he noted bullet holes in the tail unit, but Ginger held up his thumbs to show that he was all right.

'Watch your flying,' commanded Biggles crisply. 'We can't afford crack-ups here.'

'Sorry, I was in a hurry,' said Ginger, jumping down.

'I know—that's when you make mistakes. Bear it in mind. I hear the Japs are at Shansie.'

Ginger's eyebrows went up. 'How did you know?'

'One of Li Chi's spies just came in with the news. It is a fact, then?'

Ginger nodded. 'Too true.'

'Away goes my plan for busting the embankment and spilling the water.'

''Fraid so.'

'What happened to you at Shansie?'

'Nothing very much—except that I had the shock of my life. I got there all right, and seeing that the rice had been cut I was going down, thinking Marling had fixed the landing ground like he promised, when some silly fool opened up on me with a machine gun. If that hadn't happened I should have landed and stepped right into it—the last thing I was thinking about was Japs. As it was I grabbed altitude in a hurry, I don't mind admitting. Looking down I spotted Jap planes parked about under the trees. Zeros, I think they were, but I couldn't be sure—I was in too much of a hurry. Some machines were starting up so I skidded out of the locality.'

'Considering you didn't land you've been a long time.'

'I did a few circuits round the jungle and explored the river for quite a way to see if I could see anything of Marling or Lalla,' explained Ginger.

'Did you?'

'Not a sign. I could see some machines in the distance, looking for me I fancy, so I came home—not direct, in case I was followed, but via the northern end of the Archipelago. I saw the destroyers. They were south of me, heading down the strait towards Victoria Point.'

'Good enough,' said Biggles. 'You'd better put some patches on those holes in your tail. Then if you like you can join me. You'll find me on the hill with Ayert. By the way, I'm afraid we've lost the *Sumatran*.'

'What!' Ginger looked shocked.

'Tug went out to have a look at her—found her hove to with a big transport beside her.'

'Heck! After all our sweat—'

'I know. It's a bad show. I don't know what we shall do about Li Chi. I may get Tug to slip out again presently before it gets dark, to see what the ships are doing—which way they're going. I must get along now.' Biggles strode off to Ayert, who had waited.

Ginger repaired his machine in the improvised hangar. Tug, who walked in before he had finished, helped him. Then, as Biggles had not returned, they walked up to the top of the hill where they found him lying in a glade with Ayert beside him, looking out to the east across the strait. The land beyond had been thrown into sharp relief by the sun setting behind them.

'We were just coming down,' announced Biggles.

'Have the destroyers arrived?'

'Yes. You can't see them now—the trees are in the way. As I expected they've gone right into the estuary.'

'Does that matter now we can't get Marling to make a breach in the embankment at Shansie?'

'I've been thinking about that. I'm not admitting yet that we can't breach the embankment. I've had a word

151

with Ayert. He's helped me to make a rough plan showing the exact position of the spot. He knows it. Apparently there are sluices for irrigating the paddy fields. I imagine these are the fields where the rice has been cut to provide a landing ground. Where did you see the Japanese plans? Here—show me on the sketch map.'

Ginger marked the spot.

'Couldn't be better,' declared Biggles.

'What do you mean—couldn't be better?'

'The paddy fields run along under the embankment. If the bank went the fields would be flooded. I imagine that if the bank went suddenly there would be a pretty serious flood. Anything on the paddy fields would be washed away. Get the idea?'

'You mean—the Japanese planes would get washed out?'

'Yes, and any Japanese who happened to be near them. Ayert reckons that four or five feet of water, to say nothing of odd crocodiles, would sweep across those fields if the bank burst.'

'How are you going to make the bank burst?'

'With a stick of bombs, I hope. I had a vague notion of doing it that way if Marling couldn't handle the engineering side of the operation. That's one reason why I held the Liberator back.'

'It would be asking for trouble, wouldn't it, flying low across what is virtually a Jap airfield?'

'I don't think so. If the machines happened to be in the air it might be awkward, but at sundown the chances are they will be on the ground. If they are on the carpet* the flood should hit them before they can get off. By busting that bank we might in fact kill two birds with one brick—wash the Zeros away and ground the destroyers. That makes almost any risk worth while. I'm going to try it.' Biggles rose. 'You two can help me bomb up.'

'What about coming with you?' suggested Tug.

'I don't mind one coming, but the other will have to stay here to meet Henry—and tell the others what happened in case we don't get back. The Gosling should be here pretty soon. If things go right the trip to Shansie shouldn't last more than half an hour. You'd better toss to see who's coming; that's the fairest way.'

Ginger and Tug tossed. Ginger won.

'If you knock the bank down how long will it be before the effect is felt at the estuary?' asked Ginger, as they made their way back to the lake.

'I don't know—it's hard to say,' returned Biggles. 'Not long, I fancy. The river should go on falling for some hours.'

'What about Algy?' asked Tug.

'All we can do is make a raid on Victoria Point,' Biggles told him. 'It's going to be a tricky business, particularly as we don't know just where Algy will be. I've discussed that with Ayert, too. He's of opinion that they'll put him the local jail. Ayert is going to pick fifty of his best men for the job. Some have rifles of their own; others will be dished out with the Jap rifles we captured at Shansie. My idea is to go across in the *Lotus*, strike the coast some distance above the Point, and march down.'

* Slang: on the ground

153

'Then what are you going to do—rush the place?'

'Probably. It all depends on how things go. You may notice that Ayert is smiling. He thinks this show is going to be a great joke. We have agreed that our best chance is to start a panic among the Japanese, if we can, and grab Algy before they have time to reorganise. The enemy is more likely to crack if he thinks he is being attacked in strength by Allied commandos, than by locals; so instead of us painting our faces black I have suggested that we reverse the process and paint the faces of our comrades white. That's what tickles Ayert. He says he has plenty of whitewash. Actually, there's a dual purpose in the scheme—I might say a treble purpose. We shan't be so likely to shoot each other in the dark—which is the easiest thing in the world in a night operation—and it should give Tamashoa something to think about. If he can be kidded into believing that the attack was made by a strong force of white troops he'll assume that they jumped across from Elephant Island; and if he believes there is a strong force of white troops on Elephant Island he'll think twice before he attacks it. He'll probably send for reinforcements. That'll mean delay, which will suit us fine. It'll give us a chance to shift some of this perishing rubber. I'm beginning to hate that word. If I get out of this mess I'll never use an india rubber* again. Come on, don't stand there grinning; give me a hand to bomb up. I want to get this job done before daylight goes.'

* A rubber for erasing pencil marks

# Chapter 16
# Sortie to Shansie

In a short while the Liberator was in the air, not heading eastward on a direct course for its objective which would have taken it dangerously close to Victoria Point, but northward, above the clustering islands of the Archipelago. Biggles held the machine low, so that the aircraft sometimes passed between rather than over the green hills of the higher islands.

On Ginger's left, as he sat beside Biggles, the sun appeared to be falling into the sea like a monstrous crimson balloon, the distortion being due to heat haze. None of the gun turrets was manned. There was no point in manning them for they were not fitted with guns. The only military equipment the big machine carried were its bomb-racks, installed for the transport of bombs rather than for operations. In the event of opposition, therefore, the only hope of successful evasion lay in speed, of which all the Liberator types have a good turn.

Biggles flew north for about five minutes, covering in that time something like thirty miles; then, after a methodical scrutiny of the sky, still flying low he turned due east towards the dark, low-lying mainland. Ginger knew why Biggles was flying low. The advantages were apparent, quite apart from the fact that as Shansie was only sixty miles distant there was little time to take altitude. By keeping low the area of hostile territory from which the aircraft could be seen was restricted, and—and this was even more important—Biggles intended to make sure of his target. The best-aimed bombs from a considerable height are apt to miss their mark. There was to be no chance of that.

With the dying sun lining its trailing edges with fingers of fire the Liberator roared across the narrow strait—at this point about fourteen miles wide—and sped on over the forest. The jungle looked grim, forbidding, in the failing light. There was no sign of life or of human habitation although occasionally the regular spacing of trees marked rubber plantations, perhaps being worked or more probably abandoned. But Ginger knew that eyes would be looking up at them, the eyes of fugitive Chinese coolies as well as enemy eyes; he knew, too, that field telephones would soon be flashing the news of the British bomber's sudden appearance to Japanese headquarters at Victoria Point. Away to the south the Pak Chan River came into view, looking like an enormous black snake winding through the jungle.

Said Ginger: 'I reckon if we hold on this course we shall pass Shansie about twenty miles to the north.'

Biggles answered: 'That's my intention. Having overrun the village I shall turn and make the bombing run on the homeward journey. That will enable us to carry straight on for home without any messing about.'

'Going to make a dummy run?'

'Not me.'

'How many bombs?'

'You can give them the lot. There won't be time for practice shots or fancy work. The thing to hope for is that the Zeros are on the carpet for the night, not in the air. If we happen to catch 'em in the atmosphere

156

there are likely to be some pyrotechnics with us in the middle of them. Keep your eyes mobile and let me know if you see anything. We're getting close.'

Ginger stared long and steadily into the grey light that had already taken possession of the eastern sky. Not a speck marked its flat surface. For another five minutes the machine roared on over a slightly undulating plain of treetops that seemed to roll away to eternity, then it banked steeply as Biggles turned south. Ginger focused his attention on the new direction. Not a machine was in sight. For the present, at least, the sky was their own. Again Biggles turned, this time to the west, so that he was running back parallel with his outward course, but some miles to the south of it. The roar of the motors increased slightly in volume as he eased the control column forward. Again the river swept into view and beside it the green paddy fields of Shansie.

'Okay,' said Biggles crisply. 'There she is. Take station. Don't bother about sighting. Unload when I give you the word.'

Ginger took his position and, looking through the open bomb doors, saw trees flashing past below. They ended abruptly at the river and open cultivated country, across which some men were running, pointing, gesticulating, for the most part towards aircraft that were dispersed under convenient trees. Ginger saw one man stop and take deliberate aim with a rifle. Where the bullet went he did not know; nor did he care; he had little fear of being hit by such a shot, anyway. The aircraft altered course the merest trifle. Biggles' voice came clear and sharp over the inter-com. 'Ready!'

Ginger waited, thumb on the bomb release.

'Now!'

Ginger's thumb jammed hard on the button and the bombs went through the hatch like a string of sausages, taking up that curious oblique flight that bombs make when they leave an aircraft. There was an instant of suspense during which a line of tracer shells flashed past the Liberator's port wing. They did no damage. Lying prone Ginger looked down to observe results. He could see several bends in the river, but he did not know which was the right one. Flashes told him, then smoke, billowing clouds of smoke. The aircraft seemed to soar bodily as blast struck its under-surfaces. At first the smoke obscured everything; then from under it appeared what seemed to be an ever-widening ripple. It did not look dangerous or even alarming; but he knew that this was water; that the river bank had gone and that a liquid wall several feet high must be surging across the paddy fields. Men were running. Without any spectacular display of power the tide overtook them, when they merely disappeared from sight. But the force of the flood could better be judged from the way the water lifted the aircraft when it reached them; it rolled them over and over as if they had been paper models. Ginger's view of this satisfying spectacle lasted only for a few seconds; then the picture drifted away aft and forest once more filled its place. He went back to his seat in the cockpit.

'Okay,' he announced. 'The embankment got the groceries. You must have scored at least one direct hit judging from the way the waves went bubble-dancing across the fields.'

'I should be a dim type to miss a target that size

from that altitude,' returned Biggles evenly. 'I'm going home the way we came.'

The Liberator swung a little to the north and raced on over the forest, so low that the slipstream set the treetops waving, towards a sun that was now half sunk in the western ocean. Nothing opposed its progress. As it shot across the coast some fifteen miles above Victoria Point, Ginger relaxed a little. Sea and sky were empty. Or were they? A few seconds later he leaned forward, concentrating on something that had caught his eye on the surface of the water a trifle to the north of their course.

'What's that?' he asked, pointing.

Biggles' eyes found the mark. 'Looks like a dilapidated *kabang*. Probably another of Li Chi's spies coming across with more gen.'

'There are two men in it,' observed Ginger.

'What of it?'

'They're waving.'

'So I see.'

'They seem excited about something.'

'Maybe they're afraid we're Japanese, going to shoot them up.'

'Edge a bit closer,' requested Ginger.

'I've no time to hang about,' answered Biggles. 'I'd rather get my wheels on the runway before the light goes altogether.'

Ginger stared hard at the little craft for as long as it was in sight. 'Do you know something?' he queried in a puzzled voice. 'I believe one of those fellows was Prince Lalla.'

'What!' Biggles looked interested for the first time. 'What gave you that idea?'

159

'There was something familiar about the figure of one of them, and his face was certainly several shades lighter than the other.'

Biggles looked concerned. 'Lalla might have escaped when the Japanese took over Shansie. It's no use going back—we couldn't pick him up; but it might be a good thing if the Gosling has arrived to take it out and have another look. If it did turn out to be Lalla you could pick him up.'

'I'll do that,' asserted Ginger.

The Liberator landed and ran on to the shelter. Tug was there, waiting, with Henry Harcourt. The new Gosling rode in the mooring prepared for it.

'How did it go?' called Tug.

'Okay,' answered Ginger, and made for the Gosling.

'What's he going to do?' demanded Tug, turning questioning eyes to Biggles.

'There's a native craft making for Elephant Island. He thought he saw a friend in it,' explained Biggles. 'What about the ships—did you find 'em?'

'They've parted company,' reported Tug. 'The big ship is heading north-west, flat out, judging by her wake. The *Sumatran* is coming this way.'

Biggles nodded. 'If she's coming this way it looks as if she's got a Japanese crew on board—probably making for Victoria Point.'

Ginger took off in the Gosling.

'I passed fairly near those ships,' said Henry. 'I spotted Tug and we came back together. He gave me a lead to the lake.'

'Did the ships fire at you?'

'No.'

Biggles knitted his forehead in a frown. 'Queer.

160

There's something phoney about this ... but I'm dashed if I can make out what it is. Never mind, we can't do anything about it. Any news from India?'

'Not a thing. Oh yes—Johnny Crisp blew in yesterday hoping to see you. Said he heard you were about. He's got his own squadron now—Beau* torpedo carriers. Says if you have a party he'd like to bring his gang along to it.'

Biggles smiled. "Fraid he's a bit too far away.'

As the sun dipped below the horizon the Gosling returned, and ploughing a stormy furrow across the smooth surface of the lake ran on to the shelter.

'Bear a hand!' shouted Ginger from the cockpit. 'I've got Lalla and Melong. They've both been hit.'

There were several minutes of careful activity as Lalla and his overseer, Melong, were helped to land. Lalla, it turned out, was only slightly wounded, but Melong was in a bad way; a bullet had gone through his groin and another had torn a nasty wound in his side. He had lost a lot of blood. Biggles' face was serious as with the help of the others he dressed the wounds with lint, bandages and antiseptic, from the Liberator's first aid outfit.

'What happened?' he asked Lalla. 'We've heard that the Japanese are at Shansie.'

'A plane came over. We didn't pay much attention to it except that we stopped working. We were trying to make an airfield for you. But the pilot must have seen what we were doing. He went off. Half an hour

---

* R.A.F. abbreviation for the Beaufighter aircraft. A twin-engined night fighter or, as in this case, a very successful anti-shipping fighter. Armed with four cannon in the nose and provision to carry either a torpedo, rockets mounted under the wings or bombs. It carried a crew of two.

later some big machines came and dropped parachute troops on us. There was a fight but we had no chance. At the end it was everyone for himself. I took to the jungle. I'm afraid Shansie is finished.'

'What happened to your father?'

'I don't know. He was in the bungalow when the trouble began. I didn't see him. I got away with Melong. In the forest we were joined by some of our men. They helped me to get Melong to the coast. I was trying to get to you to warn you in case you flew out and landed amongst the Japanese.'

'That was thoughtful of you,' put in Biggles.

'We were shot at near the coast and I thought it best that we should scatter,' continued Lalla. 'I stayed with Melong. Some friendly natives gave us the *kabang*. We were lucky that they had one hidden.'

'Hidden? Why?'

'They say the Japanese are collecting all native craft, and taking them to Victoria Point. It may be only a rumour, but it is said that they are to be used to take troops to Elephant Island.'

'Is that so?' murmured Biggles. 'It sounds feasible.' He went on to say that he had bombed the embankment at Shansie, and why. 'Any damage we have caused doesn't matter now, I'm afraid,' he concluded.

Lalla agreed. His mood seemed to be something between blind rage against the Japanese for the destruction of his home, and despondency.

'If you feel up to it you can have a chance to hit back at the Japs tonight,' Biggles told him. 'We're planning a raid on Victoria Point. One of my officers is a prisoner there.'

'I shall come,' declared Lalla, showing his white

teeth. 'All I want now is to kill Japanese and go on killing them.'

'As far as I'm concerned you may,' said Biggles drily. Melong was carried to the native quarter and handed over to Ayert to be made comfortable.

'He die quick,' observed Ayert dispassionately, after a glance at the wounded man.

As a matter of detail Ayert was right. Melong died during the night, although the others did not learn of this until the morning, by which time the fate of Melong's son was known. The others derived some consolation from the fact that the overseer was spared the grief that this knowledge would have caused.

It was now almost dark, and Biggles determined to make his attack on Victoria Point forthwith—before, as he said, the Japanese could come to the island in the native boats, which might happen at any time, and before the *Sumatran* arrived on the scene to complicate matters.

To this Ayert agreed. His men, he said, were ready.

'Then let's get cracking,' decided Biggles.

'Can I come?' asked Henry. 'Tug says he's going.'

Biggles smiled. 'Okay. You may as well bite a Japanese or two as stay here and be bitten to death by mosquitoes.'

# Chapter 17
# The Raid

In darkness that was almost tangible, and air so heavy
with sticky heat that it felt as though it never could
have been cool, the *Lotus* nosed its way unchallenged
to the deeply indented coastline of Lower Burma. Dark
though it was the silhouette of the land was even
darker, dark with a solidity the air did not possess.
Sagging palm fronds hung motionless against the
heavens like an ornamental frieze cut out of black
paper. Nothing moved except the *Lotus* and an ever
widening ripple that started at its bows and ran back
as straight as lines drawn with a ruler to fade and at
last vanish in the mysterious gloom of the strait. The
only sound was the soft throb of the engine running at
quarter speed.

Ayert stood at the wheel, seldom moving, his whit-
ened face giving him the appearance of some frightful
pagan idol, his one eye probing the darkness ahead for
the mouth of the little river which he had asserted
would make an ideal landfall. Nor was his navigation
at fault, although the method he employed was not
apparent to the men who stood near him. Perhaps there
was no method. If there was, perhaps Ayert himself
did not know it. Perhaps he was actuated by sheer
instinct. However that may be he found the river, and
the launch, travelling noiselessly now and dead slow,
entered it like a black panther slinking into a cave that

hid its den. For a minute or two the launch went on, slowly losing way; then, without shock or jar, it scraped its side against the southern bank.

'Nice work, Ayert,' commended Biggles quietly. 'You think the launch will be all right here?'

'No one come,' answered the bosun. 'Hide here from navy gunboat many time. No find.'

'Good. Let's get along. Lead the way,' requested Biggles.

There was inevitably a certain amount of noise—the rasp of steel, the rustle of accoutrements and the patter of sandalled feet—as the commandos rose up from the deck on which they had been lying and climbed over the rail; but once ashore there was no more noise. Ginger felt a cold chill run down his spine as he looked at the whitewashed faces, hideous to behold, filing past him. They did not look much like white men, he thought, unless the faces were those of dead men. They looked more like creatures from another world.

Ayert and two big Malays led the way through the jungle. The English men came next with Lalla, and the rest followed in single file. Again, how Ayert found his way was a mystery, for there was no track; but he moved with confidence, and Biggles, who knew they were now entirely in his hands, was content to follow. He was only too glad to have a guide in such a place.

From the place of disembarkation to Victoria Point was, so Ayert had stated, an hour's march. But here his reckoning was at fault, due perhaps to frequent halts which he called while the ground ahead was reconnoitred or some suspicious sound investigated; as a result, an hour and a half by Biggles' watch had elapsed before Ayert halted, touched him on the arm, and announced that the settlement lay just ahead. For some time they had been skirting patches of cultivated ground.

Knowing that Ayert could move with no more noise than a cat walking on a pile carpet Biggles requested him to go forward alone and locate the position of enemy sentries, if any. He had a fair mental picture of the place from a map showing the main features which Ayert had provided, but the first obvious precaution was to ascertain the number and position of enemy troops. Upon this information would the direction of the assault be determined. There seemed no immediate need for haste, and his intention was, as he had told the others coming over, to spend some time getting the men in the best possible positions before striking a blow. Then, at a word, the place could be taken at a rush before the enemy could stand to arms in any sort of military order. That was what he hoped. It was a reasonable if conventional plan, and had it been put into execution it might have succeeded. But in the event things fell out differently, as in war they so often do.

The first intimation that the plan might go adrift occurred when Ayert returned in such haste that he made a good deal of noise. From the way he forced a passage through the undergrowth it was clear that he was in a hurry; and when he appeared it was at once apparent from his manner that something of extreme importance was afoot. He beckoned urgently, but all he said—in a voice thick with excitement—was, 'Quick' Without waiting for a reply, without waiting for anything, he turned and darted forward, pushing his way through bushes regardless of noise.

166

Biggles did not wait for explanations. He followed, as did the others; Ginger with his pulses racing, for he was convinced that something serious had gone amiss. He could not hazard a guess as to what it might be, but he was conscious of an atmosphere of impending tragedy, perhaps disaster. Even so, the sight that met his eyes when a minute later he burst through the undergrowth far exceeded in melodramatic effect anything that he could have imagined.

They had emerged from the jungle right in the village. At any rate there was an open space with a number of buildings clustered round it. Here, in sharp contrast to the dark silence of the forest, there was light and movement. Of this Ginger was only vaguely aware. His eyes were drawn straight to a central group of figures that in some strange way gave him an impression of actors on a stage.

There were eight men in the group, not counting a form that lay prone in a grotesque position a few yards away. There was a man who held up a blazing torch. It was this torch that provided the light—or rather, a lurid glow. There was another, a huge man, stripped to the waist, with a curved sword held above his head. And there was a man on his knees with his head thrust forward, a position in which he was being held by two Japanese soldiers. This man—Ginger stared, hardly able to believe his eyes—was Algy. It was plain that his struggles were causing a delay. The man with the sword was waiting for a chance to strike without risk of injury to the soldiers. The others appeared to be spectators. One was trying to move forward, but was being restrained. Although it lasted only for a second this picture was engraved on Ginger's brain with the faithfulness of a photographic record. And so unexpected and shocking was it that it seemed to deprive him of the power of movement. His mouth opened, but no sound came.

From this condition he was jerked with violence by an explosion within a yard of him. The man with the sword staggered slightly, but kept his feet. The point of the sword came to the ground and he leaned with one hand on the weapon while with the other he groped at his side. The soldiers who were holding Algy sprang erect. The man with the torch stood still, but his face turned sharply in the direction of the interruption. The legs of the man with the sword seemed suddenly to crumple, and with an animal bellow he sank to the ground. Out of the corner of his eye Ginger saw Biggles take a pace forward and fire again.

Just what happened after that was never clear in his mind. It was a confused picture. He found himself running forward with others, shouting. Shots rang out. Japanese soldiers appeared from houses, some armed, some unarmed, some in uniform, some in night attire. He saw Biggles shoot the man with the torch as he bolted. The torch fell to the ground and the light became dim. Henry was running after two soldiers who were making for a large bungalow. Some officers dashed out of this bungalow, and as quickly ran back inside. There was no order about anything. To complete a scene of confusion, with an incredible amount of noise the white-faced commandos surged into the picture. Ginger learned afterwards that Ayert, seeing how things were going, had called on them to charge; and this they did. Ginger stood and stared, slightly dazed, wondering which way to go. He heard Biggles' voice. It sounded angry, and it restored him to something like normal.

'The thing's got out of hand,' snarled Biggles. 'Where's Ayert?'

Ginger looked round but could not see the bosun. He saw Algy, looking completely bewildered, rubbing his wrists as he talked wildly to Tug; and, to his astonishment, he saw Major Marling, followed by Lalla, running towards the big bungalow. They both carried rifles.

'Why, there's Marling,' said Ginger stupidly. 'Where the deuce did he come from?'

'He was here with Algy,' snapped Biggles. Then he shrugged his shoulders helplessly. 'No use trying to do anything with this mob now. We'd better look after ourselves.'

Algy strode up. He, too, seemed angry. 'I'm going to get that poodle-faking admiral,' he raged, and snatching up the executioner's sword tore towards the bungalow.

Biggles shouted to him to come back, but apparently he did not hear. By now the noise was indescribable.

'Everyone's gone mad,' rasped Biggles. 'We might as well go mad too. Come on!' He ran towards the bungalow.

Fighting was now going on everywhere. On all sides men were running, yelling. Some were wrestling on the ground. *Parangs* and rifle butts were rising and falling. The air was full of noise and flying bullets. Ginger saw a Japanese officer dash out of the bungalow and streak for the forest. He did not get far. Half a dozen commandos converged on him and he went down under whirling rifle butts. A number of Chinese coolies had

169

appeared from somewhere and were rushing about striking indiscriminately with shovels and all sorts of agricultural implements.

Ginger allowed Biggles into the bungalow which he saw at a glance had been used as a military depot. Here, too, pandemonium reigned. Japanese were dashing in and out of doors and windows with yelling commandos at their heels. Major Marling was there, sitting in a chair with a rifle held like a shotgun, taking shots at Japanese as they crossed the room from one door to another. Seeing Biggles he announced cheerfully, 'Five so far. Like potting rabbits, by gad.'

Biggles grabbed Ayert as he ran past. 'I want you,' he said crisply.

'Jap man's chop head off Melong's son!' shouted Ayert, who seemed beside himself.

'I'll chop your head off if you don't listen to me!' shouted Biggles. 'This place is worse than a madhouse.'

It is doubtful if Ayert understood, but he stopped, breathing heavily. Biggles told him to collect his men and get them in some sort of order.

'You'll never stop them now; they're berserk,' said Marling casually. 'The trouble with these chaps is they tend to get out of hand.'

'*Tend* to get out of hand!' cried Biggles with bitter sarcasm. 'They're like a lot of wild animals.'

'Why not?' said Marling cheerfully. 'They're having the time of their lives,' he added. 'Leave 'em alone for a bit—they'll mop the place up for you.'

Algy burst in, eyes wild. 'Where's Tamashoa?' he demanded belligerently. 'I can't find the skunk. I want him.'

'Okay, help yourself,' said Biggles. 'I give up.' Henry

appeared, driving in front of him at the muzzle of his pistol a Japanese officer who cried aloud in English that he had always been a friend of the British—or something of the sort. The Japanese are supposed not to know fear; but it struck Ginger that if ever a man looked thoroughly scared it was Henry's prisoner.

'Found him trying to burn the contents of the safe,' said Henry.

'I know that rabbit!' cried Algy. 'He speaks English. He's the interpreter. He's one of the bunch that sent me out to have my block knocked off.' He addressed the prisoner with harsh precision. 'Where's Tamashoa?'

The interpreter did not argue. 'Gone,' he answered in a voice pitched high with terror.

'Gone where?'

'Penang. He attends a conference.'

'What about?'

'The forces on Elephant Island.'

'Don't tell lies.'

'He was gone in automobile only a minute before the battle starts,' asserted the prisoner desperately.

'I think he must be telling the truth or we should have found Tamashoa here,' put in Biggles. 'It looks as if it's his lucky day.'

Before anything more could be said on this subject Tug came in, his shirt torn and the light of battle in his eyes. 'What's going on?' he asked.

'Don't ask me,' returned Biggles. 'And don't you go off again,' he added curtly. 'Have you seen Lalla?'

'He was outside a minute ago making cats' meat of a Japanese who tried to crack his skull with a gun. Why?'

'Only that I'm going home,' answered Biggles. 'I've

got what I came here for and that's enough. We'll set fire to this place and get out. Collect any books and papers you can find and bring them along—they may tell us something.' He turned to the door.

# Chapter 18
# Li Chi Comes Back

Algy's rage seemed to have subsided somewhat. 'You were just about in time,' he told Biggles. 'Things were beginning to look extremely dim. They were just going to chop my head off.'

'So I noticed.'

'Did you know I was here, or was it an accident?'

'We knew,' answered Biggles. 'I didn't know the major was here though. Nor did I know anything about this head chopping or I should have been here earlier. It shook me when I saw what was happening, I can tell you.'

'Not so much as it shook me, I'll bet,' said Algy warmly. 'Now you know what Tamashoa does to prisoners who won't talk.'

Biggles nodded. 'The fellow must be an absolute swine,' he said in a disgusted voice. 'You can tell me all about it when we get back. Are you all right?'

'Right enough. The major's wounded though—had a bayonet poked through his leg.'

'Nothing to speak of,' interposed Marling calmly. 'Clean forgot all about it in the excitement. Where's that confounded boy of mine?' He crossed the room to an open window and looked out. 'Here, I say, come and look at this,' he went on.

Biggles strode to the window. It overlooked the

estuary. 'The destroyers!' he exclaimed. 'By thunder! We've done it!'

'They've taken on a queer sort of list, haven't they?' observed the major.

'They're aground,' answered Biggles. 'Good thing for us they are, too. Phew! What a target they'd make, helpless on their beam ends. There are the *kabangs*, too. We heard the Japanese were getting them ready to invade Elephant Island.' He beckoned to Ayert and pointed at the small craft now lying high and dry on the mud. 'Get your men together and tell them to knock the bottoms out of those *kabangs*,' he ordered. 'Be quick. We'll meet you outside.' After Ayert had gone he turned back to the others. 'Let's get out of this while the going's good. No sense in overdoing it. The Japanese may come back.'

'I doubt it,' said Marling. 'There weren't many here, you know—not above forty, I should say. Some are away at Shansie and others are out on patrol.'

'We'll get back all the same,' decided Biggles. 'Bring the prisoner along, Henry. Maybe he'll do some more talking.'

But the prisoner had ideas of his own about this. Suddenly, with the speed of despair, he took a flying leap through the open window. Ginger, who was still holding his pistol, took a snap shot at him but only succeeded in knocking a chip off the sill. Jumping to the window hoping for a second shot, looking down he saw that the wretched interpreter could not have chosen a worse moment for his attempt. Ayert and a number of his men was on their way to the *kabangs* and the Japanese had landed in the middle of them. His cry of fear was cut off by fierce yells of exultation.

Ginger turned away quickly. There was nothing he could do about it.

'He didn't get far,' he told Biggles. 'He nearly jumped on top of Ayert. He'd have done better to jump on a tiger.' He glanced at the major. 'These men are savage,' he observed.

'Of course they're savage my boy,' replied the major sharply. 'So would you be savage had you lived here and seen your friends carved up. Why, half an hour ago that infernal rascal stood calmly by and watched Melong's son decapitated.'

From outside came a noise of banging and thumping as the commandos joyfully disposed of the invasion craft. Biggles gave them a few minutes, then went to the window and called Ayert. 'Get your men together,' he ordered. 'We're going home before those sailors on the destroyers find some way of getting ashore. Any man who stays behind will have to get home as best he can. We can't wait.'

'What's the idea of the white faces?' asked the major.

Biggles told him.

'You'll succeed in your purpose,' declared Marling. 'Any Japanese who manages to get away to save his face will swear that the post was attacked by a thousand Europeans.'

'I don't think many will get away,' said Lalla, who now joined the party.

After that it was largely a matter of routine. With ferocious threats and some delay Ayert managed to re-muster his men, for although all resistance had ceased they seemed in no hurry to leave. A searchlight coming into action from one of the destroyers hastened them. Casualties, it was now ascertained, had been light.

Only five men were missing although several were wounded. These made light of their wounds and laughingly declined medical attention. The general atmosphere was that of a picnic, and the behaviour of the wounded rather like that of children who are stung by nettles.

'Don't worry about them,' advised Marling carelessly. 'They'll slap a lump of cowdung or a handful of bruised leaves on their wounds and be all right in a week. Don't ask me why the wounds don't turn septic because I don't know.'

The march back to the *Lotus* was made without incident, although towards the finish the major had to accept assistance on account of his wounded leg. To Biggles' annoyance, the unruly commandos, flushed with success, abandoned all restraint, and from time to time the forest rang with laughter as some man described a personal adventure.

'Don't worry,' said Marling to Biggles. 'Any odd Japanese who happen to be about will run the other way when they hear this din. They don't like *parangs*. I do. It's a nice weapon, particularly for jungle work, and it takes a good man to face up to one. The War Office might do worse than make an issue of them to commando troops. It's the head they're laughing at.'

'Head?' queried Biggles. 'What head?'

'They've got a head for a trophy, a souvenir of the occasion. They're passing it round . . . great joke.'

'What!' For the first time Biggles really grasped what the major was talking about. 'I'll stop that,' he declared.

'I wouldn't try—you might lose your own. They do things without thinking when they're in this mood.'

Biggles steadied himself and walked on. 'Who's head is it?'

'Apparently it belonged to that spy fellow, Pamboo.'

'Of course, he was at Victoria Point,' murmured Biggles. 'I was so taken up with other things that I forgot all about him.'

'Why worry?' said the major carelessly. 'Nothing like removing a man's head from his body to prevent him from causing further mischief.'

Biggles smiled wanly. 'I can't argue against that.'

'Everybody fights a war his own way,' asserted Marling. 'That's the Malay way. This is their theatre as much as ours, so who are we to quibble?'

'There's something in that,' acknowledged Biggles. 'But I don't like loose heads about.' He marched on.

Everybody was in good heart when the *Lotus* was reached, for the expedition had been a complete success. Under Biggles' firm orders embarkation proceeded quietly. When all were aboard Ayert took the wheel and the launch crept away into the night as noiselessly as it had appeared.

Rather more than an hour later, with a crescent moon rising out of the sea, after cruising down the western coast of the island the *Lotus* turned into the little cove that had provided so secure a berth. An instant later a shout, shrill with alarm, came from the look-out. It brought the officers, who had been resting on the deck, to their feet, swaying as the *Lotus* yawed when Ayert spun the wheel to avoid collision with a big dark shape that loomed suddenly ahead.

Biggles reached the rail in a stride. 'Watch out!' he exclaimed, in a voice brittle with alarm. 'It's the *Sumatran*.'

This dramatic announcement was followed by a brief period not far removed from consternation. It was assumed naturally that the ship was in enemy hands. Even Biggles did not question this foregone conclusion, and remembering that the *Sumatran* carried deck armament he was shouting to Ayert for full speed out of the vicinity when a hail came floating across the water to bring him round in a posture of incredulity.

'That was Li Chi's voice,' he asserted wonderingly.

The hail came again.

'It *is* Li Chi,' vowed Ginger.

'What the deuce . . . !' For once Biggles was completely at a loss. He stared at the larger craft apprehensively, as if suspecting a trap; but he answered the hail and asked Ayert to close with the ship. In a minute or two after a cautious approach they were alongside.

'What are you doing?' called Biggles, above a babble of excited conversation.

'Waiting for you,' came the answer in Li Chi's voice.

'What's gone wrong?'

'Nothing. For once things have gone right,' stated Li Chi, who could now be seen looking down from the rail. 'Come aboard and I'll tell you about it.'

'I still don't understand it,' muttered Biggles, as he accepted the invitation, having told Ayert to proceed to the shore when they were aboard.

In a few words, with his hands tucked into his sleeves, Li Chi explained, and Biggles no longer wondered why he had failed to guess the reason for the *Sumatran*'s return. Things had happened that were hardly to be expected.

'I was just getting out of the danger zone, as I thought, when we sighted a big ship hull down over

178

our port bow,' said Li Chi. 'I turned away, but she quickly overhauled us and made a signal that we were to heave to. We had no choice but to obey. Then, as she came up, I saw with joy and amazement that she was flying the white ensign. She was the *Lochavon Castle*, an armed merchantman, out from Perth, West Australia, for Calcutta. At the point where she intercepted us she was off her course, but her skipper told me that he had received a radio signal from the Admiralty to pick us up. And do you know for what purpose?'

'I couldn't guess,' murmured Biggles.

'To take over our rubber and proceed direct to England with it.'

'Well, I'll go hopping,' breathed Tug.

A smile broke slowly over Biggles' face. 'Good for the navy,' he observed. 'Somebody has done some quick thinking—but then, the navy's good at that. What about you, Li Chi?'

'There were no orders. I fancy it was supposed that I would take the ship to India. The captain thought that was the intention. But as I say, there were no orders, so I decided to come back for another load of rubber—why not?'

'That was noble of you,' commended Biggles. 'What did the skipper say about that?'

'He said the *Sumatran* was my ship and I could do what I liked with her. He wouldn't be looking whichever way I went. So I handed over the rubber. He went on. I came back,' concluded Li Chi simply.

'This is the biggest slice of cake we've had so far,' asserted Biggles. 'If we can shift another thousand tons of rubber we shall be half way home. We could never have got the job finished otherwise. We've sort of stirred things up on the mainland.'

'Ah,' breathed Li Chi. 'The raid was a success?'

'Couldn't have been better.' Biggles gave a short account of the landing, and the rescue of Algy and Major Marling—who stood listening. 'Time is what we're up against now,' he went on. 'We always were, of course, but after this things are going to buzz. Tamashoa will be really sore. Singapore, and perhaps even Tokyo, will sit up and take notice when they hear about it. They'll attack us by land, sea or air—perhaps a combined operation. It may take them a day or two to organize, but we've got to get really busy. I suggest, if you are willing, that you load up again with rubber and push off before the fireworks start.'

Li Chi agreed that this was obviously the thing to do. He said he would get the work in hand forthwith.

'We'll have another conference presently when we've had a clean up and a rest,' said Biggles, and with the others, went ashore in one of the *Sumatran*'s boats.

The Liberators should start coming in tomorrow morning,' he resumed, as they walked up the hill. 'From dawn we'll start one hour patrols in a Lightning to take care of the *Sumatran* and see the Liberators safely in. The other Lightning can stand at ready in case it is required. I'll take first shift. Until then we'd better put in some blanket drill.'*

---

* RAF slang for sleep.

# Chapter 19
# The Pace Grows Faster

Dawn found the work of loading the *Sumatran* still proceeding under the tireless eyes of Li Chi—not so quickly as on the previous occasion, for casualties reduced the number of men available and the others were resting in relays after the night's exertions. As soon as it began to get light Biggles took off in a Lightning and did a high patrol for an hour, watching the mainland for hostile aircraft which he felt sure would try to interfere. None came however.

'I don't understand why they haven't sent anyone out, but they haven't, and that suits me,' he told Ginger, who relieved him. 'I can only think that all their available fighters were washed up at Shansie and they're a bit nervous about sending reconnaissance machines.'

'I should say it's more likely that there's one dickens of a flap going on ashore,' returned Ginger. 'They're probably working out the best way of getting at us.'

'May be,' agreed Biggles.

Ginger took off, and Biggles went on to the bungalow where he found Algy, Tug and Henry, half dressed, all looking a trifle the worse for wear, sitting on the verandah. Major Marling and Lalla, they said, seemed to be having a private conference inside.

'How long before the *Sumatran* can get away?' asked

Algy. 'She's asking for it, isn't she, sitting there in broad daylight for all the world to see?'

'There's nothing we can do about it except hope that the Japs stay at home,' replied Biggles. 'She won't get away this side of noon. Get yourselves squared up—all of you. You look like a salvage dump. The fact that you're off a regular station doesn't mean that you can sit and bind like a bunch of store bashers. There's a Liberator in the shed doing nothing. Get it loaded up. Henry, take it to India. As soon as it's unloaded send it back. The other machines will be here presently. Tug, relieve Ginger when he comes down.'

The three officers thus admonished retired hastily.

Still no enemy machines appeared, but Biggles insisted that the protective patrols be maintained.

At ten o'clock the first Liberator arrived from India, flown by Angus, who reported that Bertie, Taffy and Tex, were following. The machine was loaded and taken back to India by Tug, leaving Angus on the island to rest. No sooner had the aircraft left when Bertie arrived. His machine was turned round, loaded, and taken back to India by Ginger. Taffy landed soon afterwards, closely followed by Tex. After some delay Taffy's machine was flown back by Algy, who took with him written and verbal despatches for radio transmission to Air Commodore Raymond.

The delay was caused by certain events that had so much bearing on the situation that they had to be incorporated in Biggles' reports. They began when Li Chi came up to the bungalow for a cup of tea. He mentioned that he had been in the *Sumatran's* radio cabin, and that the sky was stiff with signals, mostly Japanese, but as they were in code he was unable to say what they were about. He had kept a record of them however, in case Biggles cared to pass them on to Intelligence Headquarters, India.

'Just a minute,' said Biggles. 'Where are those books and papers we grabbed last night at Victoria Point? I'm thinking particularly of those that were in the safe. There's a chance that a copy of the Japanese secret code may be amongst them. There must be something important, anyway, or that interpreter chap wouldn't have been so anxious to burn them.'

The documents were produced, but as of course they were in Japanese they conveyed nothing to Biggles, who handed them over to Li Chi. There was no code book, but there were a number of documents that had been decoded, which came to the same thing, for they provided Li Chi with the key.

'We'll get this information to India right away,' declared Biggles. 'You'd better look through your notes, though, Li Chi, in case there's anything that concerns us.'

Li Chi got busy, and was soon able to announce that there was quite a lot that concerned them. Briefly, it amounted to this. Penang had reported to Singapore that the aircraft stationed at Victoria Point had been destroyed by a sudden flood. Biggles smiled at this, for he noted that nothing was said about Shansie, or how the flood occurred. Obviously, Tamashoa was still trying to 'save his face.' But Biggles' smile faded when Li Chi continued. The raid on Victoria Point was thought to be of such importance that it had been reported to supreme headquarters at Tokyo. The upshot of this was, two transports, each carrying a battalion of troops, were to be sent north from Singapore for an immediate attack on Elephant Island. They were to pick up Tamashoa on the way. He would take charge of the operation.

'That means the best part of two thousand troops,' muttered Biggles, biting his lip. 'My word! We *have* started something. Well, we can't do anything against that crowd—not if they once get their feet on the beach.' He unfolded his service map—a large scale map of the area. 'You know these waters,' he went on, speaking to Li Chi. 'Which way will these transports come?'

'The direct way, I imagine,' answered Li Chi, drawing a line on the map with a pencil. 'They aren't likely to go round the outside of the Archipelago—it would take them too far out of their way. They'll come up the inner channel.'

'We can watch them from one of the Lightnings,' said Biggles, thoughtfully. He was looking at the map. 'If they take the inner channel it means they'll have to pass between Lakar Island and the mainland.'

'Of course.'

'It doesn't look very wide.'

'Between two and three miles. The actual passage is narrower.'

'Plenty of water there, I suppose?'

'Plenty. All coastal ships use the channel.'

'These transports are coming from Singapore. How long will it take them to get here?'

'That will depend on the speed of the ships. Allowing for a stop at Penang to pick up Tamashoa they should be here in not more than three days.'

'That channel sounds like an nice place to chuck a few mines,' remarked Angus, who was listening.

'The trouble is, we haven't any mines; and if we had we haven't equipment for mine laying,' Biggles pointed out.

'What a shame,' sighed Bertie.

'How about borrowing some mine layers from some place?' suggested Tex practically.

'I don't know about that,' answered Biggles dubiously. 'We can't start slinging mines about on our own account; the navy might have something to say about it, particularly if we sank one of their submarines. We were sent here to get rubber, not start a war of our own.'

'I'd lay the mines and tell the navy afterwards,' declared Tex.

'If everybody started laying mines to suit himself there soon wouldn't be any navy,' replied Biggles sarcastically.

'You might ask for permission to have a crack at the transports—somehow, if you see what I mean?' suggested Bertie.

'I could do that,' agreed Biggles. 'Something ought to be done about those grounded destroyers too, before the Japs get them afloat again.' He smiled. 'With one thing and another we must have made ourselves unpopular with the Japanese army, navy and air force.'

'Why not?' growled Taffy. 'Take 'em all on, I say.'

'In offering to shift this rubber we took on plenty, without any trimmings,' averred Biggles.

As a result of all this, Biggles' despatches to India comprised: first, a concise report of the events that had occurred, and a picture of the state that then existed. Second, a request that they might be allowed to suspend transport work in order to strike at (a) the troop transports, and (b) the destroyers. The first, he submitted, was vital if Elephant Island was to remain occupied. The second was an exceptional target.

'If they say no to that, it's good-bye to our island home,' observed Biggles, as he handed Algy the despatches. .

Algy set off for India, leaving Biggles on the island with Angus, Bertie, Taffy and Tex; and they were still discussing the situation with Li Chi when Ayert arrived to say that the Sumatran was loaded and ready for sea. Li Chi went off leaving Ayert on the island as before, and in a few minutes the *Sumatran* could be seen steaming westward. Biggles sent Angus up in a Lightning to provide air cover; then he sank down and mopped his face with a handkerchief.

'Thank goodness that's done,' he muttered. 'This is getting really hectic. With more than half the rubber away inside a week I suppose we should be well satisfied. The *Sumatran* was a stroke of luck. What we should have done without her I don't know. The second half isn't going to be so easy. I reckoned on a month or six weeks before the Japanese discovered us, and then another week or two before they could find out what was going on and take action; instead of which the cat is right out of the bag.'

'If they'll stay out of the way long enough to give us a breather it will be something, if you see what I mean?' murmured Bertie, polishing his eyeglass.

'There's nothing much for their machines to see now if they do come over, as long as they don't catch the Liberators arriving or taking off,' answered Biggles. 'I'm more concerned about the two transports. If we're here for another week I shall be surprised. How we're going to shift the rest of the rubber in that time I don't know. Our only hope is to prevent those troops from getting here. If they land, I'm leaving. There's nothing else we can do. It all depends now on what Raymond has to say. If he wants the rubber, then he'll *have* to let us stop those ships.'

'What about our jolly old labourers if we have to pull out in a hurry?' asked Bertie. 'If we leave them here they'll have a beastly time with the Japanese. We couldn't do that.'

'I spoke to Li Chi about that a day or two ago,' answered Biggles. 'He seemed to think there was no need to worry—but there, he doesn't worry about anything. He said these chaps can take care of themselves—hide in the forest or push off to another island; but after the way they've worked I don't like that idea. If Li Chi's junk was finished they might get away in that. Failing the junk, I suppose we shall have to consider taking them to India in the Liberators—that is, if they want to go. They may not. But we'll deal with that problem when the time comes!'

At this point of the conversation the party was joined by Major Marling and Lalla.

'I told you to stay in bed, sir, to rest that leg,' said Biggles reproachfully. 'When the next machine goes to India I think you'd better go with it, to let a doctor have a look at you.'

'I shall do nothing of the sort, sir,' replied Marling stiffly. 'What's all this fuss about my leg? We didn't bother about wounds in the old days—no sir.'

Biggles looked surprised. 'There's nothing for you to do here.'

'I've no intention of staying here,' said the major

firmly. 'I've discussed the matter with my son. We shall return to Shansie.'

Biggles looked incredulous. 'Shansie! Why?'

'You seem to forget I have my people to look after.'

'What about the Japanese?'

'To the devil with them.'

'Yes, but who's going to send them to the devil?'

'I shall, sir. From inside the jungle I shall organize a guerilla war against the scum. They'll be sorry they ever came to Shansie—yes, by gad! Nothing like sudden death always on the prowl after dark to get a man's nerves on edge. I had some of that in the old days, so I know—yes, by Jove!'

'How are you going to get back?'

'Ayert has promised to find us a *prahu*.'

'What about your leg?'

The major flared up. 'Dammit sir, I keep telling you there's nothing wrong with my leg.'

Biggles shrugged. 'Okay—okay, it's your leg—you should know. If you want to go isn't for me to try to stop you. I'll take you across to the mainland in the *Lotus*.'

'You'll do nothing of the sort, sir. You are engaged in a military operation. Your place is here. We shall go alone. The matter is settled.'

'In that case there's nothing more to be said,' murmured Biggles. 'I'll have a word with you before you go about collecting your rubber.'

'Good man. I was going to suggest it.'

Here the debate was brought to an end by the arrival of Taffy, who had been out watching the *Sumatran*. He reported that she was well out to sea. Li Chi had signalled that all was well.

'We'll have another look at her before nightfall,' said Biggles. 'For the moment that seems to be all. We may as well have a spot of lunch. Bertie, stand by a Lightning in case we have visitors. Tex will relieve you in an hour.'

The rest of the day passed quietly. Towards sunset Biggles himself went out in a Lightning to look at the *Sumatran* which, to his relief, he found still heading west at full speed. He was about to turn back when, to his amazement he saw an aircraft coming from the west. He went to meet it. It was a Liberator. Looking at his watch and making a quick calculation he noted that there had just been time for the first Liberator out that morning to get back. He flew in with the machine. In the cockpit was Ferocity.

'You didn't waste any time,' greeted Biggles, when they met on the runway.

'We just slung the rubber out of her and refuelled,' said Ferocity.

One by one, as daylight faded, the other machines came in. Last of all came Algy, to make a night landing.

'You might have waited until tomorrow,' said Biggles, as they all went to meet him. 'No use killing yourself.'

'I've got a message from Raymond, so I thought you'd better have it,' answered Algy. His eyes were heavy-lidded from weariness, but he said nothing about being tired. 'It's about the proposition you put up,' he went on. 'There's nothing doing.'

A frown appeared in Biggles' forehead. 'Say that again.'

'You're to forget about the destroyers and the troop-ships,' reported Algy. 'You will ignore everything except the rubber until you are forced by enemy action to evacuate the island, or until fresh orders are issued. That's what Raymond said.'

'I see, thanks,' murmured Biggles.

'I call that pretty good,' sneered Tex. 'Forget about the troopships, eh? We'll be blown sideways out of this dump inside three days.'

'And the destroyers! What a chance to chuck away,' growled Tug.

'We look like getting rubbed out with our own perishing rubber,' said Ferocity, with bitter cynicism. 'Trust headquarters to think of something smart.'

Biggles' eyes narrowed as he looked from one to the the other. 'What's all this about?' he asked sharply. 'You heard the orders, didn't you?'

'Yes, but—' began Henry.

'But—nothing,' rapped out Biggles. 'If orders say we're to go on loading rubber we go on loading rubber.'

'It looks to me—' sighed Taffy.

Biggles cut him short. 'How it looks to you has nothing to do with it, Taffy. How it looks to the High Command is what counts. Okay. That's all. Get these kites* loaded with rubber. There isn't room for all of them in the shelter so I shall want some of them off the teak before daylight in case a prowling Mitsubishi comes along with a basket of groceries. If that happened we should have something to moan about. Get weaving.'

Algy turned away. Knowing Biggles better than the rest he could sense his bitter disappointment. He also knew him too well to comment at that moment.

* Slang: aeroplanes

Major Marling and Lalla departed for Shansie. Biggles saw them off. He did not expect to see them again. 'If you want anything and can let me know I'll see what I can do about it,' he offered.

'We shall be all right,' returned the major cheerfully.

Biggles went back to the runway.

For the first time a full squadron was on the island.

# Chapter 20
# The Storm Breaks

For two days peace reigned on Elephant Island. In the intervals between the comings and goings of the Liberators, now running to a regular time table, there might have been no war within a thousand miles. Nevertheless, it was an uneasy peace, and an unnatural one, as Biggles was only too well aware. His eyes were turned constantly, questioningly, towards the mainland.

Work on the runway had stopped. It was large enough for all practical purposes now that every member of the squadron knew where it was, and as residence on the island seemed likely to be curtailed Biggles decided that there was no point in going on with it. He advised Ayert to keep the men employed on the junk which, he said, might be needed earlier than was expected. Reconnaissance sorties—most of them made by himself, for all pilots employed on the trans-ocean run were showing signs of fatigue—revealed that the *Sumatran* was out of danger unless she fell foul of a remote-operating enemy submarine. Arrangements had been made by Algy, during one of the operational flights, that she should now be safe-guarded by India-based aircraft.

Biggles had two worries. The first was, of course, the troop transports, which were drawing near. He had seen them and watched them from a great height.

There was nothing he could do to stop them unless he called for special equipment for the purpose, and this, in view of his orders, he would not do. The other was the embankment at Shansie which the Japanese were repairing. This had first been reported by a spy and later confirmed by air reconnaissance. He had no bombs left, or—as he told the others—he would have felt inclined to hinder the work in order to keep the destroyers where they were. Once afloat they would, he felt sure, be used against the island. Yet a request for more bombs would certainly be met with the question, for what purpose did he want them? Should he return a true answer—and he would not return any other—he would be told to get on with his job, which was the transport of rubber. He fretted with impotence. The end seemed to be approaching fast and there was nothing he could do to prevent it. By evening of the following day the transports would arrive. Should they be supported by aircraft it might be difficult to get away. One bomb or shell on the runway would be sufficient to put it out of action.

The failure of Air Commodore Raymond to make any sign that would relieve the tension strained his confidence. He could not understand it. He had never let the Air Commodore down. The Air Commodore had never let the squadron down. Was he on leave? Was he working on another operation? If not, why didn't he do something? The Air Ministry wanted rubber, wanted it badly. Pure rubber was a bottle-neck in industry. He had sent across nearly three thousand tons, but unless there was a radical change in the situation in the next twelve hours the remaining two thousand tons would be lost, for he had determined to

193

burn it rather than allow it to fall into the hands of the enemy. Tomorrow would be the last day. He would begin with the evacuation of the native workmen to other islands, in the *Lotus*, which could then be scuttled.

As the sun went down, one by one the Liberators came in. They could not return to India that night. The pilots, every one of them, were dead on their feet. Presently one of them would fall asleep over the controls, the inevitable outcome of over-weariness aggravated by strain. As the sun sank into the western ocean he took a last look at the runway, on which three of the Liberators were parked. The Lightnings were there, too, and the Gosling, all in the open, for there was no room for them in the shelter. True, they had been camouflaged, more or less, with such materials as were at hand; but this, he knew, was not enough to deceive an efficient reconnaissance pilot. It was a situation he had always tried to avoid, for the war had proved that without air superiority it was impossible to maintain aircraft within striking distance of land-based enemy bombers. Every instinct in him recoiled from having his machines out in the open, but here again there was nothing more he could do except get the aircraft off the ground, en route for India, before daylight. He welcomed the darkness, but it would not last long enough to give the weary pilots the rest they needed.

He found Algy, Bertie and Angus sitting in cane chairs on the verandah talking in low tones. Ginger and Tug lay on the bamboo floor, asleep. Algy said the others had gone inside to sleep—they could not stand the mosquitos. Not that it was much better inside.

Biggles evacuated a six-inch centipede from the

verandah with a vicious kick, and, pulling up a chair, lit a cigarette and sat down.

'I had a look at the transports about an hour ago,' he remarked evenly. 'They should be in sight of the island about dawn. If nothing happens in the meantime I reckon they'll arrive here before noon. With plenty of daylight in front of them the troops will probably land right away.'

'What do we do—try to stop them?' queried Algy.

'With what?' asked Biggles. 'If we turned out with all Li Chi's men we might kill a few Japanese, but it would be the end of Li Chi's crew and he might not like the idea of our inviting them to commit suicide. That's what it would mean. It's no use kidding ourselves. We couldn't stop the landing so why try? It would be better to burn the rest of the rubber and give Ayert and his gang a chance to slip away. In the long run they'll do more good alive than dead. I wish Li Chi was here. It's his rubber. He might be able to suggest an alternative to burning it. But I'm not leaving it for the Japanese.'

'We could get a few more tons across tomorrow morning, old boy,' suggested Bertie.

'A mere fleabite, but we'll do that, of course. Our last orders were to go on shipping rubber so we shall go on doing that as long as it is possible. I still can't help feeling that Raymond will see us through. It isn't like him to let a unit down.'

'Aye, but he's leaving it mighty late,' put in Angus.

'Sure there were no fresh orders for me at Madras, Algy?' queried Biggles.

'Not a word. Station Headquarters was my last call before I took off.'

'I see. Well, we shall just have to carry on. There's nothing more we can do without disobeying orders.'

Tug sat up and stepped into the conversation. 'I reckon we should be justified in pulling out,' he opined. 'If we wait till tomorrow we may wait too long. Those transports are bound to carry guns, and with the rest of the island covered with jungle they would be bound to open up on the lake. It only needs one shell to tear up our landing strip and we're here for keeps.'

'I think you're quite right, Tug,' admitted Biggles. 'But it so happens that our orders are to carry on.'

'Until we're knocked out by enemy action?'

'Exactly. We can't say that the enemy has knocked us out—yet. He isn't even in sight.'

'He'll be in sight tomorrow morning.'

'A lot of things could happen between now and to-morrow morning. To lose faith in the High Command is bad, Tug.'

'Haven't you lost faith in 'em?'

'No.'

'If they're going to do anything why don't they tip us off?'

'For security reasons probably. If the enemy got to know what was cooking we should be the first to suffer. But talking won't get us anywhere. You fellows had better grab some sleep. Angus, you're on the roster for the first show tomorrow. Who are the others?'

'Taffy, Henry, Tex and Tug.'

'I see. Ginger and Ferocity will cover you in the Lightnings while you get off. I'm going to roost.' Biggles went into the bungalow, kicked off his shoes, lay down on a mat and was soon asleep.

He was awakened by the roar of a low-flying aircraft.

He was up in a flash. He had no idea of how long he had been asleep, but a glance at his watch told him that dawn was not far distant. Pulling on his shoes, but without stopping to lace them, he ran out. The others, too, were astir, asking each other what was happening. Nobody knew. They all gathered on the verandah.

It did not occur to Biggles that the aircraft could be anything but hostile and his first thought was for his machines. 'Stand by to get off,' he ordered crisply, and then stared upward, trying to pick out the machine against the star-strewn sky. He could not see it, but the sound told him that it was circling. Grey light beyond the mainland told him that dawn was about to break.

'I should say things have started,' he said. 'Get the Liberators off, you fellows who are going to India. Don't show lights. No—wait!' he corrected himself as the machine overhead switched on its navigation lights, which of course revealed its position. A signal light winked.

'He wants to come in,' said Ginger.

'More likely it's a Japanese who wants to know just where we are,' grated Tug, and then ducked as the aircraft skimmed low overhead.

'It's a Marauder*!' shouted several voices together.

'Get the flares out,' ordered Biggles, and there was a rush for the runway.

Five minutes later the machine landed. With his

---

*A twin-engined American medium bomber with a crew of 6, top speed 305 mph and able to carry 4000lb of bombs. It was armed with twelve machine guns torch Biggles guided it on to the shelter end of the runway. The engines were cut. Two passengers climbed down. One was Air Commodore Raymond, and the other Li Chi. A curious hush fell when Biggles' torch revealed the Air Commodore, his uniform as immaculate as if he were arriving at an Air Ministry conference.

'Good morning, gentlemen,' greeted the Air Commodore. 'Hope I didn't give you a fright?'

''Matter of fact, sir, you did,' returned Biggles. 'We're getting into the way here of thinking all machines are hostile. How did you get hold of Li Chi?'

'The navy has taken over the *Sumatran*. They brought Li Chi into Madras in an aircraft. I found him waiting there for a lift back so I brought him along. I was coming over. Here are some of the latest newspapers—I thought you'd like to see them.'

'Er—thanks,' answered Biggles.

'Everything all right here?'

'So far,' replied Biggles cautiously.

'The Ministry is satisfied with the way things are going,' went on the Air Commodore. 'You've done well. Getting hold of the *Sumatran* wasn't on the schedule and the Admiralty were inclined to be a bit uppish at first about airmen playing at sailors, but I smoothed things over by pointing out that it had saved you a lot of work. How about a cup of tea? I could do with one.'

Li Chi called for the cook and ordered tea for all.

'I'm glad to hear that the Ministry is satisfied with the way things are going,' said Biggles softly, but with a note of sarcasm creeping into his voice. 'They are far enough away to get a comfortable view of the operation.'

'What's the matter? Aren't you happy here?'

'Not entirely,' admitted Biggles. 'We had a feeling that within the next few hours things might get a big difficult.'

'I gathered that from your report. I shouldn't worry. The great thing is to keep up the flow of rubber.' The Air Commodore looked at his watch. 'By the way, can we see Victoria Point from here?'

'You can see it from the hill, but not, of course, with any detail.'

'Then let's go up the hill,' suggested the Air Commodore. 'We should be able to see what I came over to watch.'

'Hadn't I better get my crews off to India?' questioned Biggles.

'No desperate hurry. They can go presently. They might like to stay and see . . .' The Air Commodore broke off, gazing towards the west, from which direction now came a faint drone which, rising and falling, increased swiftly in volume.

'Let's go on up the hill or we shall miss the fun,' said the Air Commodore.

Biggles picked up his binoculars and the whole party walked briskly to the top of the hill. By the time they had reached it the first rays of the rising sun were lancing the eastern sky with shafts of blue, pink and gold. All the time the drone in the west had been growing until now it was not so much a drone as a deep, vibrant roar.

'There they are,' said the Air Commodore. He looked again at his watch. 'Right on time,' he added.

The others had already seen to what the Air Commodore had referred—a swarm of aircraft flying in two perfect formations at a tremendous height. With the new-born sun lighting their metal fitments with sparks of fire the aircraft forged on through the crystal clear air, with the majesty of battleships, towards Victoria Point.

'Forts*,' breathed Tex.

'Thirty-six,' counted Ginger.

'I asked for enough—to make a proper job,' murmured the Air Commodore.

'Strewth!' exclaimed Tug.

The Air Commodore threw him a glance. 'You seem surprised to see them?'

'Yes, sir.'

'I don't see why you should be. We received the report about the destroyers. You didn't suppose we should throw away a chance like that, did you?'

'No, sir.'

Biggles smiled faintly.

There was no more talking, for the Fortresses were now approaching their objective. Faintly across the water came a sound, a thin, long-drawn-out whine. The ground beneath the leading formation seemed to rise up in a mighty cloud of smoke and fire. The earth continued to erupt for a full minute. Across the Strait came a sudden gust of wind, bearing on it a long rumble as of distant thunder.

Biggles was watching through his glasses. 'Right on it,' he reported.

'Here comes the next lot,' said Tug, in a voice slightly more hoarse from excitement.

* American-made Boeing Fortress, a four engined heavy bomber with a crew of up to eight with thirteen machine guns for defence. It could carry 12800lb of bombs

Again the earth erupted in columns of smoke and flame. Again came the wind, and the roar.

'What a packet!' breathed Tex.

'Yes, I don't think you'll be troubled by those destroyers any more,' said the Air Commodore quietly, watching the Fortresses turn for home.

'We're likely to be troubled by those, though,' said Ferocity, pointing down the Strait to the south, where two big ships had emerged suddenly from a distant belt of haze.

'I don't think so,' answered the Air Commodore. 'Let's wait a little while and see.'

Biggles took out his cigarette case. 'Cigarette, sir?'

'No thanks. I'll smoke my pipe.' The Air Commodore filled his pipe, watching the transports. 'I don't see any air cover, do you, Bigglesworth? They must be pretty sure of themselves.'

'No, I can't see any aircraft,' answered Biggles, exploring the sky with his glasses. 'Apparently they thought they could do without.'

'That's a mistake that will cost them dearly,' returned the Air Commodore, looking again at his watch.

'You're expecting something, sir?' prompted Biggles.

''Matter of fact I'm expecting a friend of yours—Squadron Leader Crisp. He should be here in two minutes.'

'But I understood Johnny was flying Beaufighters, and Beaus haven't the range?' asserted Biggles.

'For the purpose of this operation they are carrier borne,' explained the Air Commodore. 'Sounds like them coming now.'

Drowning the drone of the Fortresses came the strident bellow of low-flying machines.

'Yes, here they come,' confirmed Biggles, again raising his glasses.

'The Japanese call the Beau "The Whispering Death,"' remarked Henry.

'If that's their idea of a whisper they must be deaf,' declared Tug, grinning, as with a shattering roar twelve Beaufighters, each with a torpedo slung below its fuselage, swept over Elephant Island and raced on towards the transports. A few puffs of flak* appeared, most of it well above the aircraft.

'That's nervous shooting,' observed Biggles.

'Do you wonder,' said the Air Commodore drily. 'The gunners can see what's coming.'

The Beaufighters changed their position to line ahead. The ships were too far off for detail to be seen, but the Beaufighters appeared to dip a little, and following this, first one transport, then the other, was enveloped in smoke. When it cleared, the ships were no longer there. The Beaufighters zoomed, reformed, and headed back over their course.

'Well, that's that.' The Air Commodore tapped out his pipe and moved towards the slope of the hill. 'I'll be pushing along back,' he announced. 'I've a lot to do. Think you'll be able to manage the rubber?'

'It should be easy—now,' returned Biggles smiling.

'That's what I thought.'

The party walked down the hill. Li Chi departed to speak to Ayert. The Air Commodore took off and the duty Liberators followed soon afterwards. After seeing

* Anti-aircraft fire

them out of sight Biggles turned to those who were staying. 'Now, thanks to the Higher Command, we can relax,' he decided.

The rest of the story of Elephant Island is no more than a report of a routine operation. In the month that followed the bombing of Victoria Point and the sinking of the enemy transports all the rubber immediately available was shipped to India. As there was then no reason for remaining on Elephant Island, Biggles' squadron was recalled to Home Establishment.*

Up to that time no further offensive action had been taken by the enemy, although it was learned by Intelligence that Tokyo was making preparations for a major assault on the island, being under the impression that Allied forces were being concentrated there for an attack on Lower Burma. This, as Air Commodore Raymond asserted later, was all to the good, for it demanded the employment of enemy troops that were badly needed elsewhere. Neutral correspondents in Japan reported that Admiral Tamashoa had been killed in action in the Mergui Archipelago. Tokyo said nothing, presumably still trying to save the Admiral's 'face'; but British authorities did not doubt the truth of the report, for it was known that Tamashoa had been picked up by the transports at Penang before they were sunk by Johnny Crisp's 'Whispering Deaths.' And there were no survivors. Refugee Chinamen and Malays hiding on the islands saw to that.

There was only one event to break the monotony of

* Posted back to the UK.

flying between the Archipelago and India before the withdrawal of the transport team. One night, a fortnight after the bombing of Victoria Point, who should turn up at Elephant Island, in a canoe, but Lalla. He reported that his father's guerilla forces, to which hundreds of tribesmen had flocked, had made life so precarious for the Japanese at Shansie that they had abandoned the post. It was now possible for an aeroplane to land there. A considerable quantity of rubber was available should it be required. The High Command decided that it was required, and Biggles was to fetch it. It was expected that there would be some trouble over this, but little opposition was encountered, and the Liberators, escorted by Lightnings, brought the rubber across without any adventure worth recording.

Major Marling was still at Shansie when the squadron left Elephant Island, and there, presumably, he remains, the father of his people. Lalla accompanied the squadron to India, having obtained his father's consent to join the R.A.F. He took with him a valuable collection of rubies, which were to be sold and the proceeds handed to the Red Cross—a contribution, as his father put it, from loyal friends in Burma.

Li Chi and his supporters, unwilling to change their way of life, elected to remain in the Archipelago. Apart from wishing to finish the junk for post-war work (and here Li Chi smiled his subtle smile) they would best help the Allied cause, he asserted, by collecting more rubber for shipment at a later date. It was possible, he added naïvely, glancing at Ayert, who was singing quietly as he sharpened his *parang*, that they might collect a few more Japanese heads at the same time. Biggles told him that if he would send word to India when the rubber was ready he would come and fetch it—but not the heads.

And with that they left their strange allies; one, a self-exiled Englishman, and the other a Chinese adventurer, two men Poles apart who had been brought together by a common cause.

'As Li Chi says,' remarked Biggles, as the Mergui Achipelago faded astern, 'it takes all sorts to make a war. There are probably thousands of men like Marling and Li Chi each fighting the war his own way. Some we shall never hear of. They may not deal the enemy a mortal wound, but they can set up a nasty irritation. They may not win big battles, but they may make it possible for others to win them.'

'Absolutely, old boy—absolutely,' agreed Bertie.

*Other great reads* ✈ *from* **Red Fox**

## Chocks Away with Biggles!

Squadron-Leader James Bigglesworth – better known to his fans as Biggles – has been thrilling millions of readers all over the world with all his amazing adventures for many years. Now Red Fox are proud to have reissued a collection of some of Captain W. E. Johns' most exciting and fast-paced stories about the flying Ace, in brand-new editions, guaranteed to entertain young and old readers alike.

**BIGGLES LEARNS TO FLY**
ISBN 0 09 999740 1   £3.50

**BIGGLES FLIES EAST**
ISBN 0 09 993780 8   £3.50

**BIGGLES AND THE RESCUE FLIGHT**
ISBN 0 09 993860 X   £3.50

**BIGGLES OF THE FIGHTER SQUADRON**
ISBN 0 09 993870 7   £3.50

**BIGGLES & CO.**
ISBN 0 09 993800 6   £3.50

**BIGGLES IN SPAIN**
ISBN 0 09 913441 1   £3.50

**BIGGLES DEFIES THE SWASTIKA**
ISBN 0 09 993790 5   £3.50

**BIGGLES IN THE ORIENT**
ISBN 0 09 913461 6   £3.50

**BIGGLES DEFENDS THE DESERT**
ISBN 0 09 993840 5   £3.50

**BIGGLES FAILS TO RETURN**
ISBN 0 09 993850 2   £3.50